THOSE
WHOM
I
WOULD
LIKE
TO
MEET
AGAIN

T0266118

Originally published in Lithuanian in the collections
Siužetą siūlau nušauti, Baltos lankos, Vilnius, 2002; *Suplanuotas akimirkos,* Baltos lankos,
Vilnius, 2004; and *Šiąnakt aš miegosiu prie sienos,* Baltos lankos, Vilnius, 2010.

Library of Congress Cataloging-in-Publication Data

Radvilaviciute, Giedra.
[Essays. Selections. English]
Those whom I would like to meet again / by Giedra Radvilaviciute ; translated by Elizabeth
Novickas. -- First edition.
pages cm
An original, previously unpublished, collection of translations from Lithuanian.
ISBN 978-1-56478-859-7 (pbk. : alk. paper)
1. Radvilaviciute, Giedra--Friends and associates. 2. Radvilaviciute, Giedra. 3. Women
authors, Lithuanian. I. Novickas, Elizabeth, translator. II. Title.
PG8722.28.A33A2 2013
891'.9244--dc23
2013001690

This publication is published in cooperation with Books From Lithuania

Partially funded by a grant from the Illinois Arts Council, a state agency

www.dalkeyarchive.com
Cover: design and composition by Daukantė Subačiūtė

Printed on permanent/durable acid-free paper.

THOSE
WHOM
I
WOULD
LIKE
TO
MEET
AGAIN

GIEDRA RADVILAVIČIŪTĖ

Translated by Elizabeth Novickas

DALKEY ARCHIVE PRESS
CHAMPAIGN / LONDON / DUBLIN

Contents

The Native Land and Other Connections 7

Resurrections of Rainy Days at a Tourist Resort 18

Autumnal People 25

Required Texts 31

Awakenings 40

Hello, 48

A Long Walk on a Short Pier 63

My American Biography 79

Essential Changes 89

Those Whom I Would Like to Meet Again: An Introduction 117

The Native Land and Other Connections

On October 8, during the elections, I had to sign a declaration before they would let me vote. Then this Mindaugas, a Harvey Keitel look-alike temporarily working on the voting commission, figured out that I had been left off the regular list because I'd voted in Chicago during the Seimas election in 1996. In Lithuania, your own people can start to feel like strangers very quickly, and it takes a long time to make a stranger one's own again. A few years back, when I realized I could spend the rest of my life in America, it was fall. Silky ducks embroidered with green and brown threads swam in the Vilnelė River. Next to the Church of the Holy Mother of God in Užupis, the burdock from the Lithuanian writer Jurgis Kunčinas's 1983 novel *Tūla* was in bloom. To change one's circumstances (home is only one of them) is no great feat for a modern, rational person. You check the exchange rate. Have your cavities filled. Rent out your apartment. Compare ticket prices at LOT, SAS, and Lufthansa, and their respective menus as well—are vegetarian meals available? Before departing, you tell all your relatives what they already know: "I'm leaving all the worst things in my life behind in Lithuania." (I heard precisely this several years ago, in Chicago, from a roofer in the suburbs. In Vilnius he had graduated from the Academy of Art.)

However, a modern person and an old-fashioned one differ a great deal. They're as unlike as the coat pockets of an old man and a young one. In the old man's pocket, there's usually a worthless bus ticket—the victim of rising prices—a few crumbs, and some little tufts of wool collected in Belgium or Germany (commemorative). In the young one's pocket, there are tissues, keys, some chewing gum, and occasionally a condom (prospective). The non-modern man under-stands his native land the way Ruta understands her village in Olga Tokarczuk's novel *Primeval and Other Times*. Approaching her imag-inary village boundary, the girl stretches out her fingers, and it seems to her that the tips of her fingers disappear. Strangers who appear in the village are born at that boundary; it only *seems* as though they've come from somewhere else. The modern and the old-fashioned per-son even understand an ordinary sentence, made up of no more than a verb and a predicate—"it was fall"—differently. It was fall, the weather of memories, wrote the poet Alfonsas Nyka-Niliūnas. In the film *À propos*, returning to Lithuania in 1998, he walks the fields of his native land, and everything around looks entirely alien to him. While living in the U.S., one of the most important events of the last century—the Americans' flight to the moon—didn't make the least impression on him. The poet even thought it made for boring television, because the astronauts would never climb out onto the moon above the village of Nemeikščiai. He wrote about Lithuania: "*There* I extended nature and things, and nature and things extended me. *Here* I cannot make a living connection to either nature or things. That's what bare and absolute exile is." When you live in exile for a long time (even by choice), your native land becomes a souvenir. A tiny house in water under a glass dome. When you shake the dome, plastic snow falls (like real snow) on the cottage. A souvenir in a room (in memory) should have a strictly assigned spot; otherwise, it begins to get in the way. Sometimes people, not knowing how to live in the present tense as animals do, move in under that dome themselves. For some reason, leaving home is always purely material, whereas returning is always metaphysical. Like the river, it's impossible to wade into the same native land twice. The sluice gates have closed; new connections have been made; there's a gap between what a person experiences living in a strange place for so long a time, and what her native land might have experienced over that same period.

CANDY
The first time you arrive to work in an American's house is a bit scary. It's particularly difficult to domesticate objects in English. People are much easier. Objects remain mute until you develop relationships with them. As Nabokov wrote about one character's rented apartment, there was, in the study, a half-empty writing table with an unknown past and an unknown future. Modern people live their entire lives without ever speaking to their objects. They're never scratched by an angry chair, they don't drown in trenches of soft furniture, they aren't seduced by slippery blankets, and old mirrors don't challenge them to nighttime duels.

The old lady Candy's basement in the suburbs of Chicago was full of things like that. After a heavy rain the basement would flood with water, so the bottoms of the old Italian furniture were splintered. The life of the old woman usually divided itself by floor. Youth was imprisoned in the basement, along with her wedding pictures in old photo albums; upstairs, a serene old age watched television. It was an eerie space, and so eerie things were bound to happen. One time, after a night in Candy's house, the hands of a cheap Chinese clock started turning in the wrong direction. (Which might be, for all I know, the closest thing to a full-grown miracle I'll ever experience.) Another time, in complete silence, and with no provocation, a six-foot square landscape of an Italian monastery fell off the wall. The string that had held it for several decades snapped precisely as I, the arrival from another continent, was making Candy some coffee. When I rode the train one Saturday evening from the suburbs into Chicago, the train went *backward* for ten minutes, as though a gigantic magnet were buried under the town, pulling the cars back to their point of departure as if they were no more than metal shavings.

Candy's parents were Italians. She herself was born in America. Next to the old lady's bed hung an article about her father, reproduced from an old newspaper. He sold papers at an intersection in Chicago's Little Italy. Next to a photograph was a story about her father's great good fortune in the New World. (I visited that intersection. No more stand. Only the same streets, where now, same as then, an immigrant can turn happily in all four directions.) Candy lived in that same Italian neighborhood when she was a kid. Those were the days of Al Capone. Mafiosi were distinguished from the other Italians by their good clothes and bad manners. Candy's mother said, "If even one of them talks to you while you're walking home from school, run into any stairwell and knock at any door." I read in a book about Chicago's Prohibition-era gangsters that one of Capone's friends wore a diamond-studded belt that Capone had given him as a gift. Obviously, Capone didn't acquire such a thing without "the spilling of blood." When Capone was locked up for a year in Philadelphia for possession of a weapon, that friend, having lost his shining subsidy, offered his services to another gang. Later all the Mafiosi moved out to the suburbs. (Just like they do in Lithuania nowadays.)

Candy had been to Europe only once in her entire life. She went to her mother's home, a small town next to Rome. Her mother's brother still lived there. By then he was completely blind, but Candy said that when she saw him she thought her father had come back from the dead. And her dead father's clothes she had brought from America fit her uncle perfectly.

I asked why she hadn't wanted to stay in Italy. Candy answered that it was very beautiful in Italy, but that the country had seemed like a completely foreign place to her. In a church there she met Father Pio, who was later canonized. He gave the young tourist from the United States one of his gloves. That glove, bearing brown blood spots from one of his stigmata, now lay on Candy's dresser. It was the most important thing in the house: I was supposed to rescue it if a fire should start over the weekend. Even though Candy had been born in America, you could feel her "double identity" in the house. It consisted of random elements, not uncommon in other American homes, but here they existed in a particular combination. Sundays there were always Domingo arias. And then there was the basil and rosemary in the garden. The garden itself. (Banal association with Corleone dying among his tomatoes.) Olive oil. Thin old-fashioned stockings and Italian swearwords. The swearwords are always the last to die. In Lithuania, you could figure out the length of the Soviet occupation by counting the number of Russian curses still in use. And thereby possibly demand accurate compensation. (In Lithuanian coinage, naturally.) One time Candy swore in Italian for a very long time while she was watching a story about Clinton on the television. Then she asked in English: "All right, so he screwed her, she screwed him, why is CNN telling us about it?" Then she also asked: "Does the president of Lithuania sleep around too?" Even though I find it difficult to trust anyone or anything, I said no, he's an upright family man. "By the way," I said, "we elected him just a little while ago. Before that he lived some six miles away from you, in Hinsdale." Candy was shocked at what I'd said in my stumbling English: to the old lady it was perfectly clear that Lithuania, which is in Europe, next to Poland, couldn't possibly elect a president from the same town where her daughter bought her fresh cookies on Saturdays.

KASPARAS AND BIRUTĖ

I didn't work at Kasparas and Birutė's house for long. Kasparas and his mother sailed to New York from Plungė at the beginning of the century. Probably it was only a few days later that he sat on his mother's lap and had his picture taken, holding the end of his mother's bead necklace in his little hand as if it were the rope of a swing. Now a ninety-four-year-old man, he walked by that photograph every day, paying no more attention to it than to a doorknob. The old couple were both Lithuanian, but they only remembered a few words of Lithuanian now and were only distantly aware of *Draugas*, the Lithuanian-language paper published in Chicago. Their American daughter-in-law and their remaining son looked after them. Their other son had died in the Vietnam War. And Birutė's leg had developed gangrene. She was diabetic. Her leg was the color of a plum. A nurse who had come to the United States from the Philippines visited every day to change the bandage. She told me Birutė's leg would be amputated in a month, but the old lady didn't need to know that yet. With all her relatives left in the Philippines, what the nurse missed most was a particular fruit. She said it resembled an apple. No one in Chicago had ever heard of it. And in her parents' garden, she said, avocados would fall from the branches like pocked black grenades. The nurse didn't want to return to the Philippines, however. Her daughter had been born in the States, and there she'd just be met by a group of poor relatives with no more to offer her than a basket of that special fruit.

One evening Kasparas asked if I would like some Portuguese wine. He searched for the bottle in a clothes closet for a long time; then we drank it and listened to Sinatra's "Strangers in the Night." The port was pressed from grapes grown on the steep granite banks of the Douro River. Over there, far from both America and Lithuania, the summers are hot and the winters very cold. That's what gives the grapes their special character. Fresh wine is the color of plums. Which made me think of Birutė's leg, which was supposed to be cut off. I broke out in a cold sweat. Kasparas was looking at one wall, Birutė another. They hummed Sinatra from memory (the way eighty-year-olds back home hum folk songs). On the wall there were photographs of them dancing in some restaurant several decades earlier.

By the time they amputated that leg, I wasn't working there anymore. The old couple's daughter-in-law called and said they'd died within two weeks of each other. Then she asked me how well I knew the woman from Lithuania from whom I'd taken over the weekend shift. I said she was only a casual acquaintance. The American daughter-in-law didn't know that in Chicago weekend work like that is found over the telephone, that is, "virtually," without ever meeting the patient, even though you have to interact on such an intimate basis with their memories and their body soon thereafter. She threw that woman from Klaipėda out. One evening, stopping in at her in-laws by chance, she found the old people alone, and Birutė with her amputated leg had wet the bed. The woman from Klaipėda returned five hours later, drunk. Before leaving, she took revenge on her employers by making four hundred dollars' worth of telephone calls to Lithuania. The old lady's daughter-in-law didn't take her to court over it because she found it too humiliating. Sometimes, when I arrived on Fridays to relieve the woman from Klaipėda, I would find her in her room eating Lithuanian herring out of a jar and drinking bubbly pink Italian wine. Her denim shirt would be tied in a knot under her breasts—she was prepared for a wild weekend with other Lithuanian immigrants who were free for a few days from their American patients. Before getting into the car, she would show me the latest photographs her loved ones had sent from Klaipėda. She said she missed her son and husband a great deal. She hadn't seen them in three years. (Still, of all the men she had to leave behind, the woman from Klaipėda would clearly miss Ben Franklin—he of the hundred-dollar bill—most of all.)

ALICIJA

Alicija came to Chicago when she was six years old. Her new surroundings bore no resemblance to her native land. Though, actually, there was the Bobak's Sausage Company store not far away, where you could buy cream wafers, pickles, cabbage, all kinds of herring, and a lot of other familiar things. The names of the children in her class were Mexican. The old Americans who had remained in the neighborhood were called "white trash." When her mother walked her to school and turned to go home, Alicija would start crying. She didn't know the English for left or right, up or down, black or white. The world, as if it were made of rubber, threatened to shrink to the size of an eraser. Every morning before class, standing with the other students, she would recite the Pledge of Allegiance without understanding a single word. The teacher smiled. She smiled even when Alicija cried. Every couple of months, in some public school, children would shoot other children. On the television Alicija would see mothers hugging one another and weeping in front of the camera. The locals would leave flowers on the school fence where the shooting occurred. There would be a very long close-up on those flowers. Alicija thought that the children in those schools shot the other children because they had to smile when they wanted to cry.

Broad-faced Mexicans with carts would drive by Alicija's house. They would sell mangos full of juice as sticky as honey, corn mounted on a stick so it would be easier to gnaw, and sliced papayas, whose black seeds shone like giant caviar. A small truck playing music would drive by from time to time as well. You could stop it anywhere and buy yourself ice cream. On warm nights lightning bugs flew about in the dark street next to the house. It seemed to Alicija that her invisible aunts and uncles from Poznan, with cigarettes burning green in their mouths, were zooming up and down the sidewalk. Her mother missed those aunts very much. In the evenings her mother would be in a bad mood. Because she cleaned Americans' houses, and her back hurt, and because she had nonetheless to write only cheerful letters to her relatives. "Be glad you decided not to return . . ." "Since you left, nothing has changed in Poland . . ." "I'm blind with envy for you . . ." That's more or less how her relative's replies would begin. One time her mother cried while talking to someone back home on the telephone. An aunt had died in some village. She couldn't go to the funeral because she had only seven hundred dollars saved up, and wouldn't have been able to fly back to the States. Later, Alicija would learn that almost every immigrant fails to bury their loved ones. Later still, she'll be in an American funeral home: everything will look like a birthday party, at least the way they were celebrated in Poznan, except that the birthday boy or girl is lying in a coffin. Her mother will tell her that when the old lady, the American she took care of on weekends, was dying in her arms, she yelled for her relatives on the second story of the house to come down, but they were too afraid. Her mother will say that to stand next to a dying person and afterward close their eyes is called "old-fashioned" here. Alicija will then get upset that her mother can't pronounce such ordinary words without an accent. Even the word "water" would give her mother away as a foreigner. After two years of school, Alicija will learn how to fold a paper flower in class. Her mother will ask Alicija to demonstrate. Alicija will say, "You take the paper, fold it in half, turn up the corners, and even them out." Her mother will ask her to say it in Polish. Alicija will say, "You take the paper, take it in half, take it like this, and then take it like that." After a few years it will seem to Alicija that speaking Polish is like climbing into the house through a window when the door is wide open.

Alicija will come to like eating French fries alone at the fast-food restaurant next to her house, watching through the window how cheerfully the black bus drivers change shifts. On the bag her food comes in is a drawing of clouds and something about the food being the best in the world.

Alicija will visit a theater where only Shakespeare's plays are put on. After the play, while everyone is applauding, from somewhere up above, a portrait of Shakespeare the size of a sail will descend, wearing a Michael Jordan T-shirt. On a class field trip, Alicija will go to the Art Institute to see Degas paintings and sculptures brought together from all over the world. She will like the women combing their hair best. It will seem to her that combing their hair was the peak of those women's development. She will go to the Museum of Science and Industry with her mother. Alicija will finally see the part of the Apollo ship the Americans first rode to the moon. Alongside all the other artifacts, there will be a bottle of brandy; the astronauts had taken it along and brought it home again unopened. (Her mother will enjoy watching a live chick breaking out of its egg the most.)

After a few more years, Alicija will start understanding television news anchors, despite the speed at which they speak. She will see that whenever bombs start exploding somewhere in the world, or there's some despot trying to claim another country's land, most often things don't begin working out until America interferes. During those years, almost all her relatives in Poland will try to win green cards in the lottery. Some will succeed. And when they come over, they'll even live for a bit with Alicija and her mother while they look for an apartment. (They'll say to her mother that they left all the worst things in their life behind in Poland.) And Alicija will understand that the whole world is here. You just need to succeed. Not be like her mother, eternally cleaning houses. But Alicija will still dream of Poznan for many more years—most often the courtyard of a five-story apartment building, the shining tramway rails, and poppy seed cake. The same cake they used to sell at Bobak's. Right there, around the corner.

POSTSCRIPT

The summer I came back from America for good, my daughter got a wart on her foot. The doctor, who cured warts with a laser, said that if it were her own child, she would try curing the wart with tetterwort juice. It takes patience, but there would be no need for anesthetics, which apparently do terrible things to the memory. (I find nothing so frightening as whatever might harm the memory or the sight.) Tetterwort, it turns out, grows everywhere in Vilnius. Particularly in old courtyards. Almost every evening for two months we picked some in the courtyard of the Basilian monastery. Nyka-Niliūnas, the one time he returned to Lithuania, wrote that he too visited the Basilian courtyard, brutally neglected by God and man, which "utterly stunned me with its mysteries as dense as the granite walls." I've known for a long time that a place can be described as accurately by an impression as by a fact. (If the poet hadn't lived in America for forty years, his impression most likely wouldn't have contained the words "brutally neglected.") Another poet, Adomas Mickevičius, who spent half a year imprisoned in this same courtyard, was exiled for all time by order of the tsar, and was never able to return to Lithuania again—not even once.

My girl sat on the boards and poked at her wart with a broken-open tetterwort—the orange juice turns black on the skin. My mother told me that her mother had told her that you can heal warts with a linen string. You should tie as many knots in it as there are warts and bury it under running water. When the string rots, the warts will disappear. A nightingale sang on the Basilian's bell tower. At six o'clock in the evening. In the middle of Vilnius. It smelled of fresh-cut boards.

I knew I would feel the same way standing in many of Vilnius's other courtyards. As Günter Grass said about memory, all the sluices were open. "Everything was right there again, within reach." There really was a giant magnet buried underground, holding me here as easily as a metal shaving. One's native land is nothing more than this connection . . .

A few decades ago, the Basilian courtyard smelled like washed (and unwashed) wine barrels to the little Ričardas Gavelis. Back then, children found German telescopes in the basement of the church. There were no nightingales singing in the tower; someone was raising pigeons there. He developed a real hatred of those birds. The pigeons, in revenge, gifted the aging writer with a bird's eyelids and stare. At approximately the same time, my uncle was learning English and Spanish in that same courtyard. The dean of foreign languages at the Pedagogical Institute was a Jew. The freshmen always tried to follow him to one of the bathrooms without stalls, so that the barriers between them and the greatest secret of Jewish manhood would fall down like a pair of pants. The dean, due to his secret's disproportionate size in relation to his height, would try to hide it with both hands. Seeing that was a real education.

The church really hadn't changed much since those days. In the silence, the frescos crumbled and fell into where all the buildings in Vladas Drėma's book *Lost Vilnius* went. I stretched out my hands, but my fingertips didn't disappear . . .

The next fall, with the frescos of the Basilian Church as a backdrop, my friend, an Estonian from Tallinn, will take a photograph of both her own child and mine. We will not have seen each other since 1991, when political analysts wrote that the Estonians too would fight for their native land to the last drop of Lithuanian blood. I'll remember this when my Estonian friend arrives. But I won't say anything. Her boy's father is married to another woman. But my Estonian friend will still be carrying that man's photograph stuck in her notebook. A photograph from a financial newspaper—he's the owner of a large clothing firm. His firm has stores in Vilnius too, but the Estonian says they're too expensive for her. The boy poked his father's picture in the notebook with a needle. I will keep the picture of both our children with the backdrop of the Basilian courtyard in my kitchen for a long time, next to a certain other souvenir. That souvenir is a clear plastic dome with Chicago's skyline beneath it. When you shake the dome, plastic snow (like real snow) falls on the skyscrapers.

Resurrections of Rainy Days at a Tourist Resort

I was about five years old the first time I was in Palanga. The streets of the town didn't remind me then of a stage set for a play about tourists, but now, in June, they certainly do. The town is deserted. The actors, having finished acting out the sorts of passion that can only be aroused in rented wooden vacation houses, are resting far away, backstage, far from the sea. The town is deserted. Real rain is pouring on the decorative villas. Real wild strawberries are blooming everywhere. Cotton curtains, crumbling like waffles in your suitcase after a long journey, hide damp rooms. You don't need to see; you remember what's inside them: walls colored with oil paint, mattresses on springs, and bare electrical wires and outlets (more likely to bring to mind the *kommunalka* of Stalin-era films than childhood). There are tennis courts next to the abandoned sanatoriums/stage sets, spotted with patches of leftover red gravel and the occasional umpire's platform that hasn't fallen down yet. When a place intended for intense activity becomes neglected, the sight of it makes one sad and anxious at the same time. Probably because the absence in it is so tangible.

When I was five, next to those same courts, my friend tickled the bare foot of an umpire up on his chair, right in the middle of a match. Keeping his eyes on the match and without taking the whistle from his mouth, he asked, "Want to get it in the teeth?" At the time, and in many situations afterward, having an excellent sense of self-preservation, I simply remained an observer. My friend now lives in America, by the way, with very sturdy teeth, even if they aren't hers, and likewise in a resort by the seaside. Her own teeth began melting like snow when she worked in the Far East, because the water there didn't contain fluoride. At intervals thereafter, her teeth's nerve endings had to be pulled out and ground down to supposed nonexistence; finally, she got a set of porcelain jaws put in. After something like that, a person truly becomes an other. It's like being reincarnated into an artificial version of your own face. I dream of perfect teeth myself, but I happen to think that if the Inquisitors of Spain have also been reincarnated, they've come back as dentists. How else can you explain those signs, those four teeth—drawn the size of melons—next to nearly every dentist's office in Lithuania: invariably

18

molars, invariably with two roots, one with a red arrow sticking out of it? You're given to understand that if you don't immediately open the door to this office, that red pain will settle into the other root too, and then even deeper, into everything that's still alive in you and so can still be hurt. It would be far better to hang up a sign showing four sliced melons, each grinning with black seeds.

There by the ocean, my friend eats salmon and probably plays tennis herself now. To me, tennis players always seemed the most stylish of athletes. Likewise, to me, Nabokov always seemed the most stylish of writers who played tennis: "This time the ball bounced sufficiently close. Franz threw himself forward, raised his racket like an axe, struck, but nothing happened." (*King, Queen, Knave,* from the original, Russian version.) Those novels, even those sentences, in which nothing much happens, are extremely meaningful because they're free of events treacherously pushing the text toward reality. Despite the fact that reality does have some rather unexpected connections to art (like sex to children). Nabokov's comparison of a tennis racket with an axe appears for three reasons: the similarity of the gestures involved; because Franz plays clumsily and with difficulty; and then—most importantly—because even in that sentence, the reader (not knowing why) remembers that Franz is playing this game with his lover's husband, whom he has just about decided to murder.

One is threatened with many forms of disgrace, playing tennis. Sometimes the ball disappears. Someone swings a racket (like an axe), the ball flies over the fence, and not even its impudent yellow is enough to save it from the great beyond. You can wade through the dandelions past the court until dark: it's not there. This leaves all the players with a strange feeling of mortification. Which is always the case when things disappear before your eyes—combs, erasers, a shoehorn, or the sandwich you just buttered.

It's best to stay at a resort for seven days, six of them "sincerely" rainy. (I stole that "sincerely" from a neighbor of mine. It was raining like it meant it then, too. I smuggled the word out of her house like a kleptomaniac with spoons in her pocket.) When it's raining, you start counting time not in hours or minutes—as do people who work too much, or people condemned to death—but rather in bursts of remembering the responsibilities you're ignoring, in clouds of distractedness, in books that must be read for the third time. Joseph Brodsky was correct in observing that reading a tedious book is not much different from doing nothing at all, so far as boredom is concerned; and nowhere is this more true than at the seaside.

By chance I happened to arrive at the same vacation lodge in Palanga where I had spent three days of my honeymoon a number of years before. The wallpaper hadn't changed. The days—yes. Water started leaking through the ceiling one night; I set the vegetable drawer from the refrigerator under the drip. Actually, the lodge had changed in little ways: a couple of luxury rooms had appeared, along with a Chinese restaurant featuring "delicious dishes created by a chef from Peking." Its small, staunchly damp tables with chairs leaning face down against them stood empty all week. One day, when the sun peeked out, the chef brought out two large (flying) saucers of his own cooking and ate outside—alone, with a sad expression. An ant ran over his hand. He brushed it off with a quick gesture, or, more accurately, erased it like a tiny hieroglyph.

Solitude, images, and smells become more intense in the rain, just like when you have a high fever. Going down a side street toward the sea after dinner, one is quite capable of considering "a spider and a little tree" to be one's acquaintances, as does a character in *The Idiot*. The rain-washed moss beyond the town looks luminescent. Through the sparse pines in the forest you see a bicycle leaning against a tree. From a distance, it looks silver, jeweled—belonging to Nobody. You have an unpleasant thought, and so raise your eyes up into the tree's branches. Nothing hanging from them but suicidal raindrops.

You can smell seaweed before you can see the water. Returning to your room and closing your eyes, you can conjure it for some time yet, even on a dry, dusty street. After swimming through the waves for a half hour, returning to shore makes you queasy with relief. You feel like a child playing a video game: "I reached the fifth level, and I still have three lives left." But if you don't swim in the sea, you never feel your body. All of its positive feelings drained away by four decades of pessimism. Although in general there may be too many bodies at a resort. You could even describe resorts as places for turning souls into bodies (and shopping into fucking, forces of nature into smoked turbots, amber into medallions). The same transformation occurs on the pages of some magazines, I've heard. There's a story going around about the magazine *Stilius*—I hope it's not true. Apparently they had to write an article about the manager of a certain company to go along with a big ad she'd ordered. However, this manager didn't have "beach clothes as thin as onion skins," she didn't "skip breakfast every day in favor of a morning run," she hadn't "decorated the pretty curve of her shoulder with an exotic tattoo," and her garden pond wasn't occupied by "a carp with golden fins." The anxious photographer out in the provinces called the home office and said, "It's impossible to get a decent picture out of this." His editor reassured him, "Look, we'll bring the manager a dress, hair, teeth, and nails. Then you'll get your picture." Incidentally, I once met a famous conductor and television host in Palanga. People differ from their photographs in *Stilius* the same way that an original differs from its forgery.

Back when I was five, I myself saw how the soul turns into a body—saw it in great detail, and from very close up. My grandfather was in a public toilet. The toilet was next to the path running to the sea, among the lilac bushes. I was waiting for him. A man was standing in the shadow of the bushes. I thought he was waiting for his woman. In a certain sense, he was. As soon as my grandfather disappeared into the toilet, the man unbuttoned his fly and, looking me right in the eye, showed me what some feminists call their childhood trauma. Then that particular body turned around and retreated down the sidewalk. As best I could, I conveyed the details of event to my grandfather when he reemerged. He, shouting "Police!" started chasing the man. Then a policeman jumped out from behind another bush (!?) stuffed the martyr of the lilacs into the cab of a garbage truck going by, and climbed in after. I don't know what rights were granted to members of the exhibitionist minority during the Soviet years, but the policeman probably released the body in question around the next corner.

In those days, Palanga's wooden villas were full of people, prestige, and Climat perfume. In the evenings on the pier, dressed in what was considered haute couture here (and in Czechoslovakia too), the ladies would show off a golden sunset of their own; as it happened, semi-precious stones from Egypt had just then started to come into fashion. Decent, law-abiding people, people who were a part of the Soviet system, would travel to India, Egypt, and other countries. Sometimes even entirely normal folk did too, I mean the sort of people who didn't mind "shaking hands with their enemies." The atmosphere of those days had somehow been miraculously preserved by the tower of the Žuvėdra Spa (now called the Feliksas). One rainy day I climbed up to the top, picked up the binoculars left on the sill, and spent a long time sailing in the open ocean along with a tiny boat in the distance.

Spending a week at even at the most ordinary of resorts nevertheless transports you into another state of being. You consciously seek this, but it comes unexpectedly, when it comes. And there's one condition—there can't be anything around you, neither friends nor enemies, only memory, with whom you strike up a collaboration. Then, like Prince Myshkin, you find yourself approaching down a dark lane. You feel like a roll of film, your images being developed. You're transparent to yourself, and therefore not of interest. To passersby, you're invisible. To acquaintances, you're unrecognizable. An obstacle on a snail's trail. A bowl in which to pour scents, snatches of conversation, colors. This dematerialized state should be relaxing, but for some reason it turns into strenuous work. It seems I'm watching everyone, but me, I'm only being watched by God. Those are the times I find myself really beginning to question my faith that God doesn't, after all, exist. For example, when at twilight in the park I find a tennis ball on the path. Without explanation, without reason, without a tennis court or Nabokov. As if it had been dropped by a cosmic juggler who'd gotten bored holding onto his ball in the great beyond, tossing it from hand to hand while riding on his tiny, silver, bejeweled bicycle. (It's only when it's "sincerely" raining that a bicycle, leaning against a pine on shimmering moss, looks like Nobody's.) You always find God in the details, but only when you have time. As the Americans say, "If there's no God, who pops up the next Kleenex?" Of course, joking like that is a sin. And to pick up that tennis ball and to put it into your purse "for all time," is a(sin)ine. There's too much in your purse as it is. (Its most precious cargo being a small child's note: "I love you.")

I usually can't remember how I get back to the city from the seaside. But this time there was an incident. Between Kaunas and Vilnius I was sitting in a roadside cafe. There was a pond visible through the window. A huge fish swam to the surface of the pond and stopped there, considering—was it better below, or up in the great beyond? A child approached the pond. With a slow shiver, the fish dived back down into the deep (surely he'd reached the fifth level and still had three lives left).

When I got home, objects were sitting about in an orderly fashion. They'd clearly been expecting me. I must have mentioned it out loud on the telephone before I left. Sometimes, when I return home unexpectedly, perhaps because I've left something behind, I come across objects in the most unlikely places, insolently strewn about the room, and there's a peculiar smell in the air, as though they'd thrown an orgy and I'd caught them in the act—the fact that they had just now been up to something sinister evidenced, for example, by the crooked runner, that apple adventurously balanced on the edge of the table, and the graying cornflower petals fallen on the cake (besides which, ten minutes earlier, I had, I believe, left somewhat more cake behind than is awaiting me on my return).

At home I emptied my purse. I poured the sand out of it and put back the pencils I'd need for work tomorrow. I fed the pregnant neighborhood cat, who is expecting kittens by her son from last year. I made some coffee and sat down to a week's worth of unread newspapers.

. . . Six ministers have been forced to resign. The premier refused to step down. Then he stepped down. The candidate for his office traveled to Moscow to celebrate an acquaintance's seventieth birthday. Secretly. Before noon, he lied about it. After noon it became clear that he had lied. He had gone because of "a matter of grave national interest." One member of our parliament offered to shoot all the others. Bush let Putin know he would have to reconcile himself to NATO's boundaries coming nearer still. The Hague Tribunal welcomed Milošević into his new jail cell most hospitably. "Crumbs of party coalitions were left on the country's political table." But the Dalai Lama arrived for a visit on Saturday, and praised the great strides taken by free Lithuania.

I took a sip of coffee and tried to understand what these truly important, by-no-means average events meant to my essentially frivolous, lazy, tourist-resort life.

Autumnal People

When I was a child, there were these candies with the brand name "Autumnal." Although they had a reputation for being good quality chocolate, they would often wind up wadded in the back of your mouth for ages, like something you worry is too close to the mark to say to someone you care about. There were other, similar candies, like the ones called "Sporting." Both cost one ruble eighty kopeks a kilogram. From the outside, both candies were very similar; only the filling was different (in color and smell). When they would arrive in brown corrugated paper boxes, people would buy them up at once, like any of the other "shortage goods" glittering in the shadow of Brezhnev's eyebrows.

People too can be divided into two categories: autumnal and sporting. And the appearance of autumnal and sporting people don't differ at all; it's just the "filling." Autumnal people understand the present as the past, while sporting people understand it as the present, or else as the future. This sort of thinking prevents autumnal people from enjoying all sorts of activities and adventures, because at the very beginning of an adventure, they always see its end (which is to say, by way of analogy with their own past experiences, or those of other people, or those in books). In short, when going for a driver's test, they already see themselves flattened in an accident. Despite this, they're always trying to have adventures, all their lives, experiencing them mostly in their imagination: virtual adventures, but with "all the bells and whistles"—tachycardia, feelings of joy or guilt, obsessions (real) and orgasms (literary), despair . . . adventures they sometimes carefully hide from strangers and sometimes show off with true masochism. On the other hand, the sporting types actually take part in adventures. With their muscles, instincts, strength, body, and blood. They jump from adventure to adventure like a hero chasing a villain from the roof of one train car to the next—without injuring himself, naturally: completely unharmed, open to new experiences, and not even, relatively speaking, all that tired.

To the autumnal among us, the past fills up a great number of empty vessels: Sunday streets in large cities, apartments with no loved ones at home, that moment of darkness on the television screen when you change the channel, cool churches on stuffy summer evenings. The autumnal visit churches to talk to themselves. (The sporting go, if they go at all, only to talk to God, and most often they only use words they've picked up in some book.) The autumnal can enjoy a cup of coffee with the dead just as much as they do with the living. Sometimes they go out to eat with them during their lunch break. Sometimes, like necrophiliacs, they even go to sleep and wake up with the dead. But at funerals, autumnals just get in the way. Only the sporting can take part in funerals. This is because the autumnal don't see the situation in the same way—they go on thinking the deceased is still alive for at least three days more. They start to remember all sorts of things from their last meeting with the person in question, and these details are, without fail, taken to have been indications that the deceased was already doomed. These people torment themselves that they weren't kinder to the deceased. As if niceness would have been enough to help the victim escape her fate. (Fate, by the way, is always sporting.) The autumnal even like to think that a golden moth flying into a dying person's room might have been that person's soul escaping, and they don't even sound silly to themselves. At the same moment, another nearby family member—a sporting type—instinctively smashes the moth between his palms. After the three nights of the wake, all the mourning autumnals have aged enough to join the "trembling hands club"; they're fit now to join the deceased in the ground, since their blood has coagulated along with the corpse's. No, the covering of the casket, the Mass, the gravediggers, the meal, all of it can only be arranged by the sporting. The autumnal don't concern themselves with anything at all: they smoke and drink, pray and cry, repeat the same things over and over, and faint dead away as often as possible.

To the sporting, art is deadly; to the autumnal, it's business (and in the early morning, it's any activity whatsoever). The sporting are brimming and boiling with energy; they can make money out of anything. For example, they could sell a matched set of perfumes for men and women, call it Twins, and sell it in double bottles shaped like the World Trade Center, handily closed with airplane-shaped stoppers. I read somewhere about a Dallas city tour in which you get driven up to the spot Kennedy died, in the same car, and get treated to the sound of the same gunfire. Without a doubt, the sporting thought up this little entertainment, but the autumnal like to ride in the car too, because they are always hunting for—are the true epicures of—powerful sensations. I'd hire only the autumnal as paparazzi (whereas, unfortunately, it's the sporting who usually get the job).

The stores in the center of Vilnius that open one day and close forever the next always belong to the autumnal (the sporting are their landlords). Sometimes, going down through the Aušros Gate (the "Gate of Dawn") on Saturday morning, I see a saleslady standing and smoking next to a display window full of Italian shoes that look like gondolas. Sad and autumnal, she doesn't feel she belongs there. I get the urge to cut her out of that background, those display shoes, like a paper doll, and paste her into a different one—in front of some black currant bushes, perhaps, with a glass of milk in her hand, standing next to two happy and dirty children. It's usually the autumnals who want to rewrite the scenario of their lives. Sooner or later (particularly in an autumn of pear yellow and wine red), they start to feel as though they aren't living how, where, with whom, or for the reasons they should. It's not that the sporting never feel this way, but they conquer such thoughts with logic, work, resolve—fishing or knowledge, basketball or beer. Single autumnal men are forever searching for the Love of Their Life. And when they find her, they get the opportunity to see how well she does without them—with the Love of *Her* Life (probably, though not necessarily, sporting). Autumnal women are true cinephiles. Normal everyday life begins to manifest a morbid sort of emptiness for them, so they take as close and personal an interest in movies as they do in their own medicine cabinets. Moving pictures colonize their brains, and then, of course, these women's meager paychecks disappear into Paramount Pictures' millions.

Autumnal people feel as though they themselves have stepped out of a film, that they're somehow different from others. Not necessarily better, but certainly not the same as everyone else. And this torments them. Sometimes they even go to a psychiatrist, until they notice that the psychiatrist—who is carefully listening to them and at the same time unraveling the sleeve of her knitting—is as much of a patient as they are. In reality, of course, autumnal people are the same as everyone else. It's just that in their desire to live more fully, to identify with something greater than themselves, they search through magazines looking to appropriate some celebrity's unusual biography, without noticing that they are nonetheless living a life very similar to their own parents'.

Sometimes the autumnal and the sporting do form couples. I saw a couple like that, street people, picture-perfect bums, sitting on a bench at the Antakalnis bus stop. The woman was sporting; the man, autumnal. He was wearing a suit, with a worn leather briefcase pressed under his arm. His eyes were focused on the distance where the trolleybuses come from. The woman attempted, with all her might, to bring him back from there:

"Come on, we'll buy a bottle of wine and sit around. Where do you think you're going, anyway?"

"I have to be at work in the Ministry at eight."

"You idiot, just because you found a briefcase in the garbage yesterday doesn't mean you work at the Ministry . . ."

The sporting always pull down illusions, turning them deftly into reality, while autumnals do the opposite. Which sort of couple lasts longer—two of one type, or one of each—is an open question. There's no rulebook. Husbands and wives, like homelands, are habits. When you separate, the most difficult thing is to get rid of the habit of communicating (particularly of communing) with your partner. Emigration is the same. And then, when people who have broken up with someone of the other type start living with new partners of the same type as themselves, after a year or two they find that half of the supposed incompatibilities they were fleeing were incompatibilities of gender, not type.

The autumnal and the sporting even use telephones differently. To autumnals, the telephone is the most intimate technology extant. You can call them in the middle of the night and start talking about whatever you like: war, the furs on sale at the Nijolė store, the cakes at Danutė's, a new brand of mineral water, the likelihood that a newly emerged pimple is syphilis . . . But the sporting have to have a reason to call. They don't like pauses; to them, the telephone is an efficient tool they use to perfection. In general, the sporting are more reliable. Unambiguous. Conscientious. Punctual. Energetic. They're not hypochondriacs; they're even optimists. They like to eat well-done meat, not cheese blintzes with vanilla. Their tree is a pine or an oak, not a linden or a willow. Their conjunctions are *and* or *also*, not *but* or *however*. Their motto is "That's the way it ought to be," not, as Leonardas Gutauskas said, "It could be otherwise, but it will never be otherwise now." Their time of year is, of course, spring, not fall.

Autumn itself has a lethal effect on the autumnal. Every year it seems to them that this fall will be their last. In the autumn, their senses become crystal clear: like dogs trained to sniff out narcotics, they can scent their morning coffee miles away—as well as coming frosts, wet wool, plaster, book dust, and a strange body's sweat, perfume, and skin. The autumnal women start to think they have nothing to wear, while the men become hungry for everything. Those autumnals who read start identifying with their texts. For at least two months those people become an autonomous nation—with their own flag, anthem, defense systems, and loneliness. All of this continues until winter. Then some weatherman comes on during the news, and he reminds us that after the second week of September (September 11, to be precise), the world will no longer be the same as it was—announcing that in many European capitals it will be cooler, and in some it will even snow.

When the first snow falls, one of my friends always eats cherry jam with the pits still in it. The tradition is a leftover from the hippie days. I try to imagine what my other autumnal and sporting friends and family will do then . . . Another close friend, now on a distant continent, will, as always, find that he's misplaced his jacket once winter comes along. Because he doesn't like (or more accurately, hates) wandering through stores, he'll buy the first one he comes across, with sleeves that are too short. And he's also forever forgetting his gloves at home and so walks around with dry, cracked hands. (I most certainly do not envy whoever might take it upon themselves to help him pick out a jacket, someday.) Yet another acquaintance of mine will defend a dissertation in which governments are treated as though they were people—all their relationships, breakups, sympathies, antipathies, strategies . . . One of my girlfriends will call late on a cold November evening—nearly nighttime—and tell me how her elderly father has again overhauled his furnace, reconnected his ducts, and done everything else that could be done in a private house to reduce the cost of heating. Then she'll add that she broke up with her lover over the phone, and instead of saying good-bye, she said, "Stick it up your ass," because he'd cheated on her. Another acquaintance of mine, a man who somewhat resembles a young Marlon Brando, will go out to eat at a basement restaurant on his lunch break and, sighing, will express a belief whose veracity he will never once ascertain during his lifetime—that faithfulness only reduces the possibility of improvement. Another girlfriend of mine will smoke a cigarette while watching the falling snow and will completely fail to notice it, and when I say she smokes too much, she'll retort, "You and your observations, it's always like getting smacked in the nose with a dry dishrag." And then, one of my coworkers, just after finding an antique Italian scarf at a used clothing store, will lament that she can only make love in their cramped living quarters when her father's out walking the dog. And someone else, whose thoughts run as straight as railroad tracks and who's given me several crushing compliments, will think he's not in my thoughts at all, and will be terribly mistaken. Actually, all of them, no matter how different, are in my (autumnal) thoughts, if not necessarily getting equal time. And now I've remembered another essential difference—for all I know—between the autumnal and the sporting: sporting people always find ideas more interesting; for autumnals, it's people. I'd like somehow to finally shake off these thoughts about them. Throw them out. Like letters onto paper, like coal into the snow. But all of the autumnals, having been accidentally distinguished by a yellow maple leaf star that's fallen onto their backs, and without being driven by anyone, are already en route to a place from which it will never be possible—no, not even by taking sedatives; not even while stroking a sleeping child or watching the most fascinating film—to return.

Required Texts

I didn't ask the most important question: what will happen if, over the course of a year, I don't manage to write that coveted, extremely well-selling novel? How will I look into the eyes of the committee—*in corpore* and then every one of its members separately—that naively believed in me and gave me a creative stipend? Even a graphomaniac, if he's sufficiently disciplined, knows it's impossible to write a "good novel" for money alone, just as it's impossible to get a "good woman" to sleep with you for money alone. You're unlikely to squeeze virtuosity out of need and speed. And what's going to happen if I do write that book after all, but it doesn't sell? Six months later they'll be selling it in thrift stores, together with copies of cookbooks brought over from Great Britain. The publisher will take a bath. Maybe I'll have to return my advance? What if the publisher's idea of a decent novel is irreconcilable with my own? Six months have already gone by. I don't have even my first sentence in mind. The first and the last sentence should be like pistol shots: the warning shot and the shot to make sure of the kill. Not that you can tell all that much from a first sentence alone—for instance, you can't necessarily distinguish a "great classic" from a contemporary novel from its first sentence alone. "For a long time I used to go to bed early . . ." How could you guess, right off, just from the words themselves, that that's the beginning of Proust's *Swann's Way*? "He dreamed a dream, and in it he seemed lifeless." That's not all that different. Perhaps even more interesting. (If it was in first person, you might even think it was from the same book.) But it's from Arvydas Juozaitis's *Laikraštis*. Well, I'll probably have to flee the country in a panic. Head for the hills, as they say. I imagine myself applying for a visa to travel overseas, and in the box where it asks about any debts incurred, I'll write: a particularly popular unwritten novel.

By the by, I should calmly and coolly tally up how I used six months' worth of my stipend. It might be a lesson to me. Twice I took a taxi to the suburb of Buivydiškės—one of my friends was suffering from a serious depression: eight three-liter jars of pickles she'd canned had exploded. And then, good grief, when I think now of all the stuff I bought . . . I bought hundred-dollar shoes because they made my feet look like a stranger's . . . a pedigreed cat, out of unforgivable snobbery (once, British cats would cost only six hundred litai; now it's a thousand two hundred) . . . my usual Ysatis de Givenchy eau de toilette (I've been using it since the day—to be precise, the night—I felt a woman). I like my perfumes to have "pedigree" too, because after two minutes on me all the others start reeking like a hip flask. And then, I bought a Zepter pot. (I keep old keys in it.) I gave three hundred litai to a friend; she's renovating a farmhouse out in the country. I took her some wallpaper out there, once—the same kind they have at the Shakespeare Hotel.

There isn't a living soul at that farmhouse in the early spring. The more I see of places like that, the more I like them. It would be nice to head out there for a day or two, with my cat and an imaginary lover . . . without any commitments. (That's what my drunken neighbor says to his wife when he comes home at two in the morning: "Dammit, Ada, just let me back in! No strings attached! Without any commitments!") We could watch the *Panorama* news hour, relaxed, luxuriating in the republic's most important facts and figures . . . Maybe they'd have some psychic on. Then, when my imaginary man falls asleep with my cat, I'll sneak out for a walk in the woods, so I don't disturb them, wearing his gloves, feeling my "hand melt inside the glove like snow." Some women's poems are just as good as a short story. (A novel, no. Most often women aren't "attracted" to this genre; they don't have the time, or the rage, or the money for alcohol, and once again, I'm terrified about my novel.)

The last time we drove out to the country together, my friend's father's shoe wound up filled with acorns and maple seed "helicopters" by some gremlin, or perhaps a marten. Walking in the silence, we found little footprints in the snow, sneaking up from the mystery of the woods, leading to the shoe. Maybe I should start the first sentence of my book with those footprints? Or maybe—with the mystery? Or maybe with how my friend was eighteen years old when her mother died? She remembers that her mother liked sunsets in Palanga, watermelons, silk blouses, mother-of-pearl clips, small children's clothes hanging to dry in the sun, and being happy.

Perhaps a real writer can't just start writing whenever she likes, but it's true that you could start with anything. From a little gray thread pressed into the three-dimensionality of a white piece of paper. Or a little hair (an eyelash?). I'm not sure. First I need to live through a little bit of life, and only afterward turn it into credible fiction. Sometimes it works out. Most often not. It's comforting to know that there are others writing in a similar fashion. A talented man once complained he couldn't begin writing a short story about his first teacher because he couldn't remember how the buttons were sewn onto her worn-out postwar coat: in a cross, or in parallel lines?

I do seem to know, at least theoretically, what a novel needs to sell: sex. Someone is lying on my, that is, my heroine's, chest—or she's on someone else's? If not sex, then at least something slightly indecent, or even some kind of wild gypsy-type erotica. "The qualities required for the birth of the erotic act—logic and firmness of mind above all, imagination, humor, and daring, to say nothing of the power of conviction, organizational ability, good taste, esthetic intuition, and a sense of grandeur . . ." (*Emmanuelle*, p. 138; I yield at once to such unquestionable authorities . . .). All of these qualities would, perhaps—one way or the other—suffice; but, as I've already said so succinctly, I need to live through a bit of life before trying to turn it into credible fiction. And the last guy I saw naked was the plaster statue of an Indian standing in the Maxima supermarket on Mindaugas Street.

A book should take a couple of good swings at God, of course. And let's not forget the aesthetics of disgust. There should certainly be mention of someone's bodily secretions. Dripping from the ear, the backs of the knees, the underarms, the genitals. And death, of course, must be present . . . but in a bravura mode, cheerfully. As in American films. An old professor with a fatal illness decides to go back to his home state for the weekend, accompanied by a college student. There he runs into a woman he once loved (older, but still attractive, dressed in nearly the same muslin dress), guzzles beer in a local bar, then—visited by miraculous powers—sleeps with the woman, and, with the sun rising over the hills of South Dakota, dies in the coil-spring bed of his childhood, watched with a smile by his student. To the student, who was a wreck before the trip, it becomes clear that life is worth living.

Maybe some episode from just after the war would come in

handy. At the moment, given the wars on the Internet and in signed letters in the newspapers, the topic is, it appears, timely again. You have to "weave" some exotica into your text. Fairy tales from distant countries, pop culture references. The reader has to wade into the text knowing he will find something recognizable. The same goes for those people whose acquaintance the reader wants to make (but only in the text). The characters too ought to seem familiar. So the reader can be a bit frightened, surprised, shocked, tickled—but never drowned. And, most importantly, don't make them sad. No, there must always be laughter. Avoid the temptation to dwell on metaphysics, transcendence, or time. Those things will still be there whether you think about them or not. (Unknown and unchanged.)

Chronologically speaking, starting my novel with its first sentence won't work. I think in a dotted line; I have no willpower. Two years ago I did start trying to put together a plan for my life, but then the alarm clock went off. I'll have to start my book from several places at once, while cooking up dumplings at breakfast.

Grandfather had a lover during the war. (Before and after the war, too, but not the same one.) This woman sometimes went to church wearing a rather "loud" silk scarf, with red and blue roses on a yellow background. She must have really stood out in the churchyard. Grandmother knew the scarf was a gift from my grandfather. One time, the neighbor ran up, all out of breath, and said, "Go pick up Juozas. He's been shot—in the barn. You know which one."

I'm guessing Grandfather had been on top. On that beloved woman's breasts. Because he'd been shot in the lungs and hip and shoulder, while she was still okay. They carried him, barely alive, to the dispensary; blood bubbled out of his chest wounds in a little stream, so no one even thought of worrying about his hip. (I saw that bullet for the first time some forty years later—he and I both did— still stuck in the bone. They'd taken an X-ray of Grandfather at the polyclinic in my hometown, just because of an ordinary case of sciatica, and found the bullet by accident.) They nursed him for a long time. My mother, while my grandmother was doing the work that is never done, balanced Grandfather's leg on her neck with her back turned to him, because for some reason his shoulder hurt him less that way, and told him stories about her friends from school to pass the afternoons. (One of these friends now lives in Germany, another in Poland, and yet another just sold her apartment in Vilnius. She's decided to renovate her parents' neglected farmstead in the country, to go there, as she said at my mother's funeral, to shuffle through the fall leaves in her boots and then die.) Nevertheless, Grandfather got up after a few months, and the very first day he could, went out. To that same lover. Later, unfortunately, they took that woman to Germany to work and . . . never brought her home. The "loud" scarf with red and blue roses—by what means, I could not say—ended up in a cabinet at home. Grandmother never wore it. She kept it for no reason, the way I sometimes keep a forgotten program from a once-memorable play in a drawer.

After the war, Grandmother had one more child. A boy. He was six months old when he died. When I asked what from, she said, "In those days . . . who really knows, my child, what he died from. Viliukas cried all the time, and the cottage was smoky." Then she'd start staring out the window. (For some reason I imagine the cigarette smoke like worn sock-rags printed with faded roses flying through the air.) The dead boy wouldn't have come to mind, or perhaps I wouldn't even have been told about him, had we not been forced to exhume and rebury him. Grandfather, nearly in his dotage, decided one day, with no provocation, to move his parents and the boy's remains to another plot, surrounded by a new fence. Two men gathered up the three sets of bones in a cloth and buried them in another spot in Užpaliai Cemetery. I was still in the first grade. The impression made on me by the cemetery remains clear. Ingeborg Bachmann (let her be yet another exotic inclusion) wrote something about "unappeasable crows and the fear of death." All that was left of that boy, I well remember, was his skull. Like a cabbage leaf, or my open palm.

Water flows from a miraculous spring next to that cemetery. And it wasn't just the people from Užpaliai who believed it was miraculous, but people from far away as well. The water bubbled like blood from the lungs of a giant shot through the chest lying under the earth. After the reburial we washed our hands in it. Strange . . . the boy was my uncle, whom, had things been different, I might call on the phone today. Sometimes when thinking about one or another death, I remember what a particularly devout professor of mine once said: "You'll rarely meet a person as evil as God."

Grandfather's old age was relatively peaceful, if you don't count his high blood pressure. He hated pigeons, grafted all the neighbor's trees, wrote complaints to the newspaper (about the pigeons too), and used to take the prettiest apples from the collective orchard to the prettiest salesgirls in the local stores. I loved him more than my father. (If I were being honest, I'd have to say I loved him even more than I did the Count of Monte Cristo.) He loved me too. He didn't tell me so; I knew it thanks to certain signs, because men like that are ashamed to verbalize their feelings. And when Grandfather was already quite old, I had a dog. The dog would take revenge on us for this or that by pissing on a corner of the refrigerator until it finally rusted out. Once he pooped on the bed—squatted there surrounded by glaciers of white pillows. Unlocking the door to our apartment, Grandfather found several hard, ochre-colored tablets that looked like quicklime. And he thought they were peanuts. In the Soviet days, there was a shortage of peanuts (and other nuts too). Grandfather put the leash on my dog, poured the tablets in his jacket pocket, and later, at home, sat down at the table and put on his reading glasses. Careful of the tablecloth, he spread a newspaper on it, and poured out his prize. He started picking at them with his nail. After a few jabs, he started muttering that these shells were very strange, the way they crumbled, and what on earth was going on?

Grandmother was the first to realize that shit is not a shell, whatever it might contain. When she started laughing, she laughed first hanging halfway out the window, then in the kitchen, then leaning on her sewing machine. And after Grandfather, without saying a word, washed his hands clean, and for some reason gave my dog—who was panting energetically—a reticent sort of look, and then went and lay down. Grandmother shut herself up in the bathroom and, burying her face in a towel, continued laughing. Obviously, it was her own tongue that set Grandfather's adventure loose among the neighbors. He didn't say a word for almost two weeks. He'd fry himself some smelts and go lie in bed quietly, calmly reading *Vilnis* and *Laisvė*, the Communist newspapers his cousin had sent from America. But when he dared to step outside and had to walk down the road in order to bring apples back from the orchard, and the neighbors sitting on the bench followed him with their eyes, he felt as if the story was tripping along behind him, taking little peanut-sized steps. Once, when I told some people the story of Grandfather's adventure, while everyone else was laughing, one person said, "Be quiet, she's talking about what kind of family she grew up in."

I find it pleasant now, if sometimes unbelievable, that all my living relatives fit in my one bed. Everyone else eats, smokes, sits, and smiles around me from photograph frames. When I look at them in the slanting rays of the sun, I feel calm. Those slanting rays of sun always seemed to me like they ought to rank as one of the wonders of the world. Next to the Colossus of Rhodes or the Lighthouse of Alexandria. Wherever they might occur—in the woods, at home, or in an old wooden shed.

"My child," I said to my daughter one night in bed, "don't get angry, but I have some sad, glad, and at the same time somewhat awkward things to say to you. I love you very much. But we're going to have to start sleeping separately. I'm not just your mother. I'm a woman, too. Sometimes, in the dark, or if you just look at my shadow, I'm quite pretty. I checked myself over naked yesterday in the bathtub with two mirrors. I say all this because I've recently found myself a friend. We'd already met, but we ran into one another again at the Vilnius Book Fair recently, and this time, for some reason, it stuck. I feel as though I can't live without him—today, anyway. I'll give it to you straight, as I would to a friend: I want him now, here, lying on my chest, just like you."

I see the eyes of this girl, who's accustomed to all my talk, turn glassy:

"What's the guy's name?"

"His name," I say, "is Bohumil. His last name is Hrabal. And if I don't read him now, I'll shoot myself. He won't be faithful to me for long. He'll melt into other women's and men's prose in various citations . . . And if they manage to use these citations in the proper places, he'll endow their texts with miraculous powers. Those texts will become enduring works in their own right, and best sellers. And those two things are practically irreconcilable. I've been wondering myself for the last six months how to reconcile them. And they're paying me good money for my thoughts. So, maybe you could go to your own bed now?"

"You should live so long," the child says, and fumbles to pull the lamp's plug out of the outlet.

It's beginning to be obvious that either my novel won't get written, or else I'll write one that doesn't sell. For the second weekend in a row now I sit in the kitchen or lie on the sofa, and instead of reading Kundera, McEwan, Allende, and Irving, instead of learning to think in a high or low style from Immanuel Kant of Königsberg or Emmanuelle of Bangkok, from Kabelka or Kubelka, I read bits of Hrabal. That book shoves me down into my bed on weekends like one of those hydraulic presses for compacting recycled paper. I read five or six pages of his last novella, and can't manage any more—I simply get worn out. I run sweating behind his sentences like a rat in Prague's sewers. That's when I set Hrabal down on my chest. I close my eyes and feel him with my entire body, as his hero once felt the naked gypsy woman lying on him. And like he did then, I don't want anything anymore, just to "go on living like that forever . . . as if we had been born together and never parted." For six months now I've been pondering how and what I should write in order for it to be liked, and look, Hrabal put it all into a single sentence: "If I knew how to write, I'd write a book about the greatest of man's joys and sorrows." Most of all I'm charmed by the subjunctive mood in this sentence. It shouldn't be there, of course, but he's not being coy. The subjunctive mood here represents the necessary, conscientious, and commonplace doubt of a person who knows very well how to do a thing or two.

For what it's worth, now I'm going to peel the bandages off my toes and put on a pair of seamed stockings. (In honor of Hrabal.) I'll pull them on slowly, gradually unwinding them, starting from the tips of my toes, so there won't be a run in their insect-wing thinness. Then I'll jump into black suede shoes and go out onto the street. Even though it's raining. Soaked through. And the streets are crooked. But in the spring, who knows, something could always happen. I could meet someone. I could meet spring itself. Or the beggar Volodia, who sometimes follows elegant women down Bazilijonų Street and parodies their mincing gaits behind their backs. Because if

I sit here in my kitchen any longer thinking about what best-selling fiction should be like, I'll start picking at my ears, which haven't been washed in six months. Like Shrek, I'll make candles out of their wax and be steeped—put so accurately!—in the intimate light of my candles. If I start thinking about best-selling fiction again, I'll go white-hot and disintegrate like a wire. After a few weeks, the neighbor and his Ada will break down the door. (Without any commitments . . .) He'll kick at my ashes and say, well, she was a smoker, and she liked to burn those stinking candles of hers, probably belonged to some sort of cult, and look at the pigsty she lived in—it could be even worse!

Yes, if I continue wondering about what sort of literature sells well, I'll feel like my grandfather on that sorry day he also sat in his kitchen, a supposed Soviet surplus scattered on American newspapers, and, to no good purpose, with his nails, searched carefully for a nut.

Awakenings

If, before dawn, I open my eyes upon waking, I see my dead mother's photograph on the wall. That's why I hung it across from my bed. The photograph was copied and enlarged by a woman artist I don't even know (and who refused to accept money for it) from a small, completely candid shot. I don't know the exact occasion of the photograph, but I believe it was somewhere, taken by a male friend of mother's on her way to the sanitarium. I was very young at the time, but old enough to hate that man. Only now is it clear to me how much that hate must have hurt my mother at the time: she had gotten divorced three years earlier, found herself someone else, and immediately after fell ill with an incurable disease. (When I think about this, I remember that children frequently meet their ends in the same way as their parents.) In the photograph my mother is sitting lighting a cigarette on a whitewashed cement mileage marker at the side of the road. Wearing a black silk dress sewn (or more accurately, resewn) by my grandmother.

My eyes open, but without getting out of bed, I say:

"Mom . . . Let's talk."

"Well, be quick about it," she answers a bit curtly. "Just until I've finished my cigarette."

"This past fall I went to Kaunas. Your granddaughter, looking out the window of the bus, saw a cow and asked, Does that cow belong to anyone, or is it Nobody's? I said, Cows always belong to someone, only people can be Nobody's. Mom . . . Now, when I wake up in a pool of sweat, most often at daybreak, I start to feel quite clearly that I myself belong to Nobody. My eyes are Nobody's. My arms are Nobody's. My legs, skin, nails, lungs, breath, and hair—Nobody's. It makes me feel terrible."

"How did your daughter's semester go?" she asks.

"Same as ever. I was at her school just yesterday. The teacher drew a diagram of their behavior and social skills on the blackboard. As four circles fitting within one another. In the central circle were the children whom everyone else wants to be friends with, sit next to, and go on dangerous expeditions with. They're the best students, too. Your granddaughter isn't there. She's in the second circle, marked with a star. The star means that at least two girls in the class don't like her."

"Okay," says mother, exhaling smoke.

"What's okay?"

"That she isn't in the center circle. I wouldn't have been in it, either, if they'd drawn diagrams for us back then."

I don't say anything. Because I doubt I'd even have made it into the second circle. I would have been in the third or fourth. (Of hell.) But even now, as my mother smokes in the world beyond the glass, I don't want to make myself out to be worse than she already thinks I am. Actually, in her eyes, I've only really done serious harm to my reputation maybe twice in my life. One of those occasions I don't even want to remember, while the other was perfectly ordinary. I was about twenty-five at the time. I didn't come home to bed. (I regret that night for many reasons, not just because of my mother.) I clearly remember how I was dressed, in a white sheer linen dress with a large butterfly drawn on one thigh (I like asymmetry in clothing and hair styles). When I came home in the morning, Mom was sitting in our small kitchen with the dog, drinking tea. Now I realize she had been there a good part of the night. (I also realize something else—I myself really have absolutely no interest in sitting in the kitchen all night waiting for my own daughter like that.) Without looking at me, my mother then spoke a single sentence: "I thought you weren't like all the others." That sentence (and particularly her not looking at me) was enough. To this day.

"Well, I'm going." She stands up, leaving the roadside marker, leans over, and with her small hand brushes the silver cigarette ashes from her black dress. Already leaving, as if by the way, she adds, "Don't get carried away. You aren't Nobody's. I'll be thinking about you . . . for at least another few years."

No chance of going back to sleep. I get up. I go into the kitchen and make a cocktail—fifteen drops of valerian and fifteen of haw-thorn in a third of a glass of water. I can drink a bucket of this brew; it helps, but only psychologically. When there's a half-hour left before the alarm clock goes off, I fall asleep. On top of that, before it has a chance to go off, the child sleeping next to me turns over on her side and smacks me in the face with the back of her hand. As awakenings go, this is actually one of the nicer ones.

It's really unpleasant to wake from a nightmare. It's been two years since the cardiologist told me the movies I was watching weren't nearly violent enough to give me a heart attack. He suggested I really focus on the coverage of the Chechen War, if I wanted to do myself in properly. And particularly those shows in which journalists ask, very professionally, lingering over each detail as though it was a mouthful of delectable cake, how the criminal of the week went about killing this or that old lady and boiling her in a pot. (In pieces.) So when they showed what had happened after Chechens took the audience hostage at a musical theater show, I watched television until the middle of the night. The worst, of course, were those bullet-riddled women who were draped on the ground and over chairs in graceful modern-dance poses. In the middle of one report, a considerate friend called and asked if I was watching the news from Moscow. "That's just exactly what I'm doing," I said. He advised me, "At least don't explain what's going on there to the kid. She won't understand, anyway. She still cries over teddy bears." I still cry over teddy bears myself, so maybe that's why I had a nightmare that night: I'm lying in a hospital. Into the room comes Putin in a white coat. (". . . the son of a factory worker who learned his manners among bullies on the streets of Leningrad and in judo classes. . ." *The Globe and Mail.*) Next to the president stand several men with IV bags. They strayed into my dream from another newspaper article, about hospitalized prisoners being brought their medication not by nurses but by FSB (Federal Security) agents. The president in his white coat approaches me, one hand behind his back; he smiles with his eyes like ice, and says: "*Popravlyaetes', popravlyaetes'*—get better." But in my ears it echoes "*Otpravlyaetes', otpravlyaetes'*—get out." I wake up when the cold barrel of a pistol touches my temple. I'm lying with my head pressing up against the metal rail of my armchair.

I go to work early in the morning. In a daze. A car drives by. On the side is a sign "*Avarinis spynų atrakinimas*—Emergency lock opening." I read it as "*Avarinis sapnų atrakinimas*—Emergency dream opening." How nice it would be to call a service like that in the middle of a nightmare—I mean, while I'm still alive. Before I'm shot dead. Before I'm heaved off a ledge to splatter in some abyss.

Before I'm suffocated by gas. Before I've choked on the water-soaked towel. In the evening I take the garbage out into the yard. "Life has become so trivial," my elderly neighbor, a former high-ranking KGB agent, who has watched the same news reports, says sadly. I can't disagree. Everything's become trivial: love, the mafia, tending the dying, lumps of sugar, prayer. Not that long ago the president of the most powerful country on earth used to end his annual speech with the phrase: "God bless America." This year George W. Bush ended this way: "May God bless our coalition."

If you have a lot of nightmares over the course of a few weeks, they collect in the brain like coral reefs. You get heart palpitations. At the Diagnostic Center, I had an ultrasound done of the organ thought to be so vital to love. But to start my treatment, I have to go to another office and pay 90 litai. I returned to the clinic, to the same doctor I'd seen two years before, and modestly, with great dignity, I spread my high-quality black-and-white ventricles and valves on the table in front of him. The doctor said, "Get undressed. Don't be so tense. We'll do another ultrasound." "What?" I asked, "You don't trust the Diagnostic Center?" "I trust them," he asserted, "I trust them so much I was even married to the doctor who did your test, when I was young. Which is why we'll do it over again." Then he continued: "I completely agree with her conclusion. Your heart is still healthy. It's the cardiogram that's bad." He pulled a book out of a drawer, opened it to a diagram of the heart that looked impressive even from a distance, and, pointing with a pencil, explained the circulation of blood through the veins (blue) and arteries (red). Wanting to distance myself at that moment, I tried to think of Kieślowski. "Put simply, you don't know how to enjoy life," the doctor said. "You can't change the world, but you can change your attitude toward it. Don't hurry home from work. Stop in a perfume store and take in the scents. As many pleasant scents as you can. Listen to music more often. Lying on the floor, or even in the street, with earphones. Mozart might help you. But loud music, or Beethoven?—no. By the way, how are your relations with men?"

"Very good," I said, thinking of men generally, as a sort of aggregate. (As half of humanity. Or like penguins in a snowstorm, huddled in a pile in distant Antarctica.)

43

"Excellent," said the doctor. "And pay attention to the drunks in the street. They usually walk alone. They haven't seen their kids in a couple of years. Their apartments are either mortgaged to the hilt or already sold. Their pants have been pissed in. Sometimes more than once. But see the happiness shining in their eyes! How sincerely they manage to enjoy each moment. Do you suppose you could try to follow their example?"

"I'll try. I'll give it my very best," I said on my way out the door.

Going to the foot of Pilies Street, I sniff through every shelf of the Kristiana perfumery like a dog (or like a bitch, if you prefer, political correctness aside). The saleslady starts following me. (Just in case.) How unjust, how rude, and what a mistake, I think, to judge a person by her worn coat. Exactly the same as judging how attractive a woman is from her perfume. As I approach the Aušros Gate, God, perfectly in tune with the doctor's instructions, sends an alcoholic. I start watching. Two well-dressed men hurry by. The alcoholic stands in front of them, or, more accurately, blocks their path with her bullet-proof purple llama-wool sweater, smiles (something compels me to count her teeth), puts out her hand, and asks for a handout. One man starts digging deep in his pockets for change. The other—at first I can't believe what I'm seeing—quickly unzips his jeans and puts his signifier of masculine power into her hand. The woman pulls back. Recovers. And out flows a long Russian-Polish monologue, which probably sends those men winging all the way to Rotušes Square. And that speech of hers is the one thing in that whole sorry scene worth our absolute respect, attention, and emulation.

Somehow—again, perhaps, God is not above lending a hand—I stumble home. Sweat runs down my back. The kid says, "Just let me finish this movie? The police will catch the guy in a minute . . ." I don't even glance at the screen; and anyway, I'm afraid of the television set too. I lie down and try to guess when I'll be woken up. After a half-hour I feel my girl, all warm, cuddle up to me. Toss and turn. Then she says quietly, "They caught him. Kicked him. And then they shot him. But Mom, I'm probably not going to fall asleep . . . I'm hurting all over . . . those damn bobbies . . ." Then I can't restrain myself: "What the hell is this all about? You know you aren't allowed to watch thrillers before going to bed. How many times have you been told? Other parents—well, other moms—don't let their kids watch those movies at all! Never. But here it's a free-for-all. Because I don't have the time, and you're completely irresponsible. And to make matters worse I started going to those German lessons even though I don't have the time for them. *Sorglos* is how you say 'irresponsible' in German, I believe. What do you expect? An hour and a half of nothing but guns and chase scenes. In those movies the police and the criminals are exactly the same sort of character, it's just that the 'bobbies,' as you call them, have the law on their side." The child's gone quiet. But she thinks it over. Then, clambering over me, she gets up, goes to the bathroom, and comes back with some cream. "Rub my back." (Then I realize that "those damn bobbies" are actually "boobies," which are hurting after her dance lessons.)

But there are calm evenings too, and calm awakenings. I like them very much. I generally do wake up a half-hour before I get out of bed. I call those thirty minutes my stolen time—stolen from the day, from my routine. You need it, not just to speak with the dead (as if they were alive), but also to gently, calmly, and respectfully remember some of the living (as if they were dead). In that half-hour—stretching to an hour or two, psychologically speaking—I rewind the movie of my life. Or, better, with the caustic developing agent of my just-awakened consciousness, I reprocess the film—go back over the important things. I remember the texts I read long ago, that helped form my personality. The men who "made" me a woman. And people who revised me like a text. Lying there, I hear the rain splattering on the window. Later, in the daytime, that sound will start reminding me of fast typing on a computer keyboard. But in that half-hour, lying under a warm blanket, I surrender to the rain gradually, with passion, in complete forgetfulness, giving it thirty minutes of true loyalty. To the point where I feel the rain on my skin. Just as I did in my youth. Even walking through an outright storm, I wouldn't take an umbrella. I didn't have between-seasons shoes, either. (I don't care for intermediaries: neither between summer and winter, nor between oil companies and the state, nor between God and man.) Now I always take an umbrella in rainy weather, because if I get sick, there's no one to look after me, and a nasty sense of self-pity, demoralizing in the highest degree, is always ready to sneak up on me. I have a whole range of extraordinarily mature methods for killing this sense. But sometimes I still don't succeed. Then I stretch out my hand and talk to the forefinger of my right hand as though I were speaking to a tiny little person who understands me and sympathizes with me (really as if I were speaking to my own body and blood). I can't claim authorship of this comforting if insane approach. The child in Kubrick's *The Shining* talked to his finger the same way.

It's been a long time since I've had a cold. Now I have other problems. In the spring I'm getting married. For the second time. I didn't think second times ever happened to women like me. But these portentous sorts of thing are always happening to me. He's an ordinary guy. (An electrician.) He exudes peace and understanding. I need the peace most of all. (Because I've got enough craziness and ill temper for both of us.) Besides (and this is particularly important), this guy isn't afraid of me. Not at all. Because he has figured me out. When the computer breaks down and won't immediately—this instant— fix itself, and I start swearing and get angry, not at all with myself for being an idiot, not even with the viruses that have ruined my work, but with this fellow here who has nothing to do with it, he seems to take some quiet pleasure in it all. And continues to want me. Right there, in the kitchen. Even like that—furious, sweaty, unshaven, and disgusting. At the same time, he's very romantic. And, for the time being, he's forgiving and has a protective streak. It's this latter talent of his (very rarely met with) that really won me over. Even now I find I resent it a little. He's constantly, considerately asking me this or that: How come you don't have fur-lined winter shoes? Or: What makes you think that soup you made didn't taste good? Or: Why did you say it's your fault that your daughter got an D in history?

I'm happy that when we recently met for the first time (in person) in a restaurant, he didn't speak the words I was so anxiously expecting. Like these, for example: You know, nothing will come of this, because of what am I—an ordinary electrician, while you're a published author . . . you write for a newspaper! He didn't say it, but wanting to head things off at the pass, I pulled out a quote, probably Tsvetaeva: "What is fame? Just a word." And he saw that I was sincere. I don't even get annoyed by his ignorance of literature. Last week I told him some more about Tsvetaeva. I don't know what time of day she hung herself, but to me it would be most believable if it were early morning (after first waking up). He said to me, "How odd . . . you see, I've always thought that Tsvetaeva slash Akhmatova was the same long-suffering Russian poet."

For now he just drives me home after we see one another. (From Švenčioneliai.) But I'm starting to panic at the thought of the day he'll move in here. I'm particularly afraid of our first nights together. (I'm thinking of all my awakenings.) I know a couple of ways to turn over in bed without waking up the person next to you, but in the long run, that gets tiring. (Even the bed gets tired of it.) All in all, if I wake up, he'll wake up at some point too. He'll turn on the light (after a couple of years, when, unavoidably, some of the spark will have gone out of things, this will be as welcome as a terrorist attack.) He'll probably take me by the hand. Without opening his eyes, he'll kiss my hair. And with his lips touching my ear, in a whisper, as considerate as ever, he'll ask, "Why did you wake up?"

Even now, in anticipation of this, the question fills me with horror, because . . . well, how will I ever manage to give him a short answer?

Hello,

Today is one of those Sundays as interminable as a piece of chewing gum. There you have a simile taken from everyday existence. Goda and the neighbor's boy forced me to go see the *Karlsson-on-the-Roof* movie. In the dark I gave the children some gum, and then I started to worry. I asked the little one, "Do you swallow it sometimes?" He admitted it: "I swallow, but not on purpose. Freken Bok says that all sorts of things happen, even in the best families. If I were to eat a couple of pieces at a time, I'd come down with appendicitis." The boy's father is an actor. They live above me. Apparently the words of strangers slosh around in a child's head as easily as they do in mine.

But yesterday was a long day too. If I was a cynic, I would have started my letter like this: The morning dawned, clear and sunny, on castration day. (But I'll save the worst for later. Like it or not, that's why I'm writing.) And I'm still terribly upset. As though it wasn't enough that in the course of a single week the washing machine bit the dust, my cordless phone gave out, and the furnace stopped venting properly . . . But unrepairable things happened too. Actually, the phone only needed a new battery. You know where I found it? Right near your favorite stomping ground, the Akropolis shopping mall. The salesman said batteries like that hadn't been made in a long time, what's the charger's voltage? I was reluctant to admit I didn't know; after all, I'd had the phone for years. (Whenever I'm in an electronics store, they address me politely at first, like they would anyone else. Then—with suspicion. By the end, they're treating me like a patient on her last legs.) The salesman said, go on home, our telephone number is on the receipt, call us before you plug the phone back in and read off what's printed on the charger, because if it can't handle the voltage, this battery will burn up your phone. Warily, I asked if I should read *everything* printed on the charger, or else . . . should I be more selective? He just waved his hand. I went home, and there, in place of one, I found two of those things . . . those chargers . . . hanging there. I got down on my hands and knees to follow the cord up from the outlet, in order to figure out which charger was the one I'd been using . . . and my purple rayon skirt tore. And not on the seam, either. I mean the one I bought at the general store in Obeliai that time. I was planning to go to my class reunion in it—I don't know which one, maybe the hundred fiftieth. They've already reserved a cafe for it—one that's already been bombed twice, as is appropriate for the city of Panevėžys.

The telephone is working now. But why that other charger is hanging there remains an "open question" (to utilize one of the political clichés of our age). My neighbor is a dead man, when he gets back. He could have fixed everything in two seconds, but he's off mushroom hunting in Labanoras with his wife and the Tyzenschnauzer. I've read, by the way, that those dogs aren't all that safe. And you can't tie them up because they go out of their minds. One bit through a child's hand, apparently. As soon as he gets home, I'll tell him. But first let him help me buy a new computer. He said he'd install three things for me, the first day—Windows XP, Word, and Woolite. Perhaps I should hurry up and thank him for the offer? Because when I say nothing, he seems to get grumpy. Then his son (a flighty musician type), without lifting his fierce little troublemaker's face from behind his newspaper, says: "No, no, you've gotta get her Linux and Clorox, *then* she'll react." But it's not funny . . .

Relations with that family are going downhill all around. Too bad. They were among the few people with whom I wasn't afraid to be myself. Not long ago we were coming home from visiting some mutual friends and my neighbor said, "You need to straighten out your disposition." He was driving. Sober. His profile was flawless, as on a coin. Like it was cut from tin plate. You could slice bread with a nose like that. I said, one's disposition isn't like a dresser drawer, waiting to be tidied up: one's disposition is a matter of control. You see, on our visit, I'd raised my voice rather unattractively (when I talk quietly, no one listens). The discussion got interesting—it was about ugliness in literature. I don't care for it . . . Neither ugliness, nor literature. It's much better to write letters like this. Literature is simply another artificial thing among all the other artificialities surrounding and congealing around us. And it's getting more artificial all the time. Lewis Lapham's table in his introduction to Marshall McLuhan's book *Understanding Media*, in which he describes the differences between citizens and nomads, can be applied equally well to traditional and contemporary texts. Dream has replaced art. And pleasure, happiness. Celebrity, successes. Passion as truth, truth as passion. Pornography, drama. Polymorphism, heterosexuality. And journalism, literature. All that awful postmodernism ruined everything. Standards were scattered to the four winds. Contexts got confused. When we say "empire," we mean the perfume; when we say "morning miracle," we mean—like Victor Erofeyev, in his essay of the same name—waking up with an erection. But I want an empire to have emperors, damn it, and walls impervious to cannon, and I want a morning miracle to be a cat licking its paws in a slanting ray of sunshine. But, you know, I suppose I'm changing with the times as well; I've started confusing criteria left and right. For example, I've started judging some poets' works by how well they take care of their children (particularly those born out of wedlock), rather than by the subtleties of their texts. And, horror of horrors, when I read their poems, they seem so terrible.

Writing an ordinary letter has turned into a pretentious pastime. It's worse, of course, if you save them all—me, I tear them up. Saving letters is like saving someone's hair. Scents waft from them—the things suggested by the particular way they chose to fold the paper, all the lurking analyses of their handwriting . . . Not to mention the things Mika Waltari wrote about: "Therefore I wrote my friend a rather foolish and impatient letter, and all my senses were agitated as I wrote this letter, so that I sent my eyes and ears and nose and the tips of my fingers and perhaps my mouth too with this letter, so that she was forced to hesitate, when she read such an impatient, irritating and disturbing letter."

A close friend wrote me a letter once when he was very ill. He w nearly blind and could barely hold the pencil in hi nd. He gave it to another person to give to me if he should die. I was in America at the e. I only found out about the letter when he was already dead. But I had the chance to see him befor died and have a talk about important things. I never d read the letter; I called the man to whom it had been entrusted and asked that he b it with t opening it.

And then, when you had finished school and were writing letters to me while I was working in a country village, they always had a double crease in them. When I was first married, I ironed my husband's slacks that way (and then he wouldn't let me iron anything ever again).

If my computer hadn't broken down, this letter would be printed on one of those sprocket-feed pages, with those edges like that ear of yours and its three piercings. But it's okay it turned out this way. You must have gotten the list of our classmates in an e-mail by now. They were supposed to send it to everyone. I have two class reunions coming up this year: one for just us friends, and one for the whole class. It was a list of all our telephone numbers and e-mail addresses. (Sorry, sorry . . . the cat just walked by, right under my nose, and spilled some of my coffee here onto the table and onto the page . . . I'm too lazy to rewrite the above; when it dries out, no doubt some of the words here won't be entirely readable . . .)

You know, I saw Linas's name on the list, and the kolkhoz appeared before my eyes. He's eating watermelon in an abandoned chapel, spitting out the cockroach-like seeds. Bats are flitting around in the nearly dark sky. We're going out to steal apples tonight. I was so envious of you then, the way you and that German Studies student were making out in a clay ditch. (Did you read that the Japanese have practically proved that life could have begun in clay?) I liked to imagine your teeth worn down from acid, because I was in a panic that no one would ever love me because of my teeth—and, in general, because of my other . . . complexities. One time, Linas, half-naked, clambered up on a crane at the kolkhoz construction site, lay down, wrapped his feet around the shaft, pushed himself off, and, looking at the red sun upside down, sang *Marina, Marina, Marina . . .* Who knows why, but I knew at that moment that he would be going away to the university, as he'd already served his time in the army. You two hardly knew one another. But you were the one he told that philology students are good for getting your exercise lying down. Wasn't it you? Well, let him rest in peace. But wait, why is he on the class list? Maybe they'll invite his widow? It wasn't long ago. Virga said that he couldn't feed himself after the stroke—they did it for him. (And not intravenously, but with purée through a tube down his nose.) Well, anyway, we'll either take a group excursion to the cemetery or honor him with a minute of silence. And while everyone's keeping quiet, in my thoughts I'll hum *Marina, Marina . . .* as I always do on such occasions. Actually, did you know that Linas's mother was completely blind? When he was a teenager, he'd cut up blankets and sew dolls out of them. He would patch their body parts together out of different textures, so his mother would get a clearer picture by touch.

You remember Aistė? That time Virga found her American underwear on a shelf at the Science Academy library? How passionate we were—well, some of us—in those days. Much later Aistė graduated from the Police Academy. Divorced now. Like you. Like me. She works at the public prosecutor's. Can't smell a thing. Thanks to chronic sinusitis, and the medicine she takes for it, she has anosmia. She even claims to be relieved about it, these days, because sometimes there are nights when two suicides need to be cut down and carted away, and she has to be in the room while the police photograph the bodies and write it up. She's taken up drinking, too. But not because she's squeamish. She hates it when you have to arrest one parent, who's done away with the other, in sight of their children. It usually happens at night. The kids see a puddle of blood, and so think the police are to blame for everything. The men who dragged one of their parents off to who knows where. They probably call someone to spend the night with the kids. A grandmother, or a neighbor. And one child opens his eyes in the dark. Like in John Irving's *A Widow for One Year*: "Tom woke up, but Tim did not."

When Virga called me and asked for my e-mail address, so she could send the list of everyone who's coming, and I said I didn't have one, she nearly cried. She said, how will we keep in touch now, I divide people into two groups, those who have e-mail and those who don't. I said, I divide people into two groups too, those who divide people that way and those who don't. She sent everything by ordinary mail.

Now when I come home late at night from somewhere or other, I hear every sound echo by my house, as though it were in a tunnel. A couple of acacia leaves stick to my shoes and climb up the wooden steps. Then drop off and stay behind. Decide not to come in. I believe it was Nyka-Niliūnas who wrote that in the autumn, time merges with space. In the fall, I imagine time like fruit in a jar. The year written on the lid under transparent tape. Time looks out at us, its little flattened pear face pressed up against the glass. If it weren't for those goddamned poets, our relationships with all these ephemeral phenomena, with the fall, and particularly with love, would be so much simpler. We'd be KO'd less often. But why have I bothered writing to you about the autumn? The seasons never affected you. And never changed you.

Now that everything's over with, I'll admit to something. After my divorce, I fell in love with this guy. I thought it was impossible. (I'm a hundred and fifty years old, and, like that café in Panevėžys, I've been blown up twice.) Maybe I wasn't in love, but I crackled with the desire to see him every day for about six months. We could talk and talk for hours—completely sober, too. I called him Karlsson-without-a-roof. One time I gathered up my courage and said, let's go to the movies. You know what my state of mind had to be for me to ask some guy to go to the movies! For me, it's the same as hanging upside down from a crane half-naked. And he said, "Two hours? With you? In the dark? . . . I can't, because . . . um . . . I'm impotent?" I hadn't been to the movies in a long time. I didn't know that they checked everyone there now, for security reasons. I went by myself, to *Sky. Plane. Girl.* The movie was okay, a chick flick, but the lack of structure bothered me. Just like I missed a more tangible basis for the insanity in *The Hours.* But Renata Litvinova was wonderful. I really liked one of her lines in particular. Or more accurately, her intonation as she spoke it. She's walking with her beloved journalist and asks, "What do you think, do I love you?" She asks it in exactly the same way a person might ask that of themselves in their thoughts. And now a year has gone by. What do you think . . . do I still love that guy who didn't go to the movies with me?

Okay—on to what I should have started with. Just don't jump to the conclusion that I've gone out of my mind on account of my sedentary way of life, like the Tyzenschnauzer tied to his doghouse. See, an American I know, who promised my kid a cat, sent along a book called *Cool Cats: The 100 Cat Breeds of the World*, so she could pick one. On the cover there's a picture of a Russian Blue, as graceful as a panther. That's what I wanted, but Goda picked a Scottish Fold. If I hadn't been so ignorant, I would have paid more attention to this sentence in the description of the breed: "The appeal of this shape [meaning those peculiar ears] is clearly that it gives the breed a more humanoid look." Indeed, all of the breed's recorded character traits are things you'd say of people as well as animals: "intelligent, sensible, sweet." Well, that's not surprising in itself. You too will have heard those crazy, love-starved women bragging a hundred times, "Our dog is so intelligent, so bright, it seems he understands everything! He's a member of our family. The only difference is, he doesn't talk!" At the cat show, the Scottish Fold looked normal. There were two other kittens in the same litter with upright ears. Apparently, you can't breed two Scottish Folds together, because if two mutated genes end up in one cat, two other pathologies show up: feet overgrown with cartilage, which makes them lame, and an immobile tail that hasn't separated from the spine. The Scottish Fold mutation was first found in a Scottish village in 1961, but the cats weren't allowed into any shows in Great Britain until 1983, because they were considered degenerates instead of a breed to themselves. They let us take the kitten home from the kennel only after three weeks, when he was fully weaned. That was when I found out that he'd been born, like me, on March 12th. We're both Pisces, so we got along perfectly from the start. For half a year he lapped warm milk, didn't eat much, and played with balls of yarn at night without making any noise. I particularly liked it when he glanced to the side—the whites of his eyes became little triangles. But, soon enough, I started feeling uncomfortable around him.

I woke up at dawn, one day. I tend to wake up several times a night, because at night I tend to devote myself to thinking about all the ways I might live a more virtuous life. Potter the Cat was lying on his back, next to me, looking at the celling, his little front feet set on top of the blanket. Without moving, I looked up to see what he was looking at. There wasn't anything there. No fly, no spider. I realized he was looking at the ceiling . . . just staring. He looked, and, as Victor Pelevin might say, saw something it was better not to understand.

Another time, I woke up early Sunday morning because the cat had stepped on the remote control and the television turned itself on. (I have no desire to write that the cat turned it on.) Turned itself on full blast. Do you know what was on? A children's show, about animals. Potter lay down across my chest and watched that show for ten minutes—eight full-grown shorthaired Persians playing in some kennel. From the side it looked like Potter was smiling (but all cats look that way from the side), and his folded ears reminded me of tiny sealed envelopes with love letters inside. And then, a few months ago, M. came over for the weekend. By then we were already catastrophically pissed off at one another. I was unforgivably rude. When I think of it now, I'm appalled. I told him he was neither spiritual nor passionate, only sensitive, and all in all, I said, he shouldn't go looking for God between some woman's breasts (I suspect he already had someone back home, and just couldn't yet make up his mind between us). He scowled, opened a can of beer, and turned on a soccer game. I went to sleep in the room farthest from him. I left the cat sitting on his lap. In the morning, M. found his shoe had been peed in (I hardly wept over this), but the cat hadn't stopped there—in the middle of the night, Potter had raked my calf with his claws, drawing blood for the first and only time . . . It was only much later, when my memory began filing the details away, one after another, that I remembered who won that soccer game M. had been watching. Or, rather, who lost: the Scots. You remember, the Scottish team and their fans were rampaging around Vilnius, spending thousands of pound sterling, walking the streets polymorphously, with hairy legs and plaid kilts . . .

In bed now, in the evenings, I read the interminable John Updike. Potter sits on my chest of drawers, pushes the cover off of my Italian wood veneer jewelry box, and winds my mother's florescent bead necklace around his leg. Holds his leg up and looks at those beads for a long, long time. Then he slowly puts down his leg and the necklace slides back into the same spot. Exactly where it was.

A month ago, Virga came to Vilnius to attend a course on public relations. She stayed at my place; I was in Kaunas with my kid at the time. After we'd both gone home, she called to tell me about her visit. She'd woken up in the night to see shining beads rising slowly from the chest. She said, I felt each hair on my head turning to wire and standing up on end, one at a time. Palms sweating, I reached under your pillow for my cell phone, to call the police, but then I remembered that your damn cat was there.

Thursday, without calling beforehand, a couple of "incorrigible" friends came by. It was past midnight before I walked them to a taxi. I went back inside and the lights were on all over the apartment (I was certain I'd only left them on in the hallway). Potter was shyly perched on the cutting board eating, in turn, either a cold potato or a pickle. Next to him there was a bottle of wine lying on its side. Not a drop left. You think he lapped it up? I suspect much worse. (He cleaned it out.)

I've started smiling without noticing it on my way home from work. I break into a grin turning into the gateway of my apartment building, and because of that I sometimes pleasantly surprise one of my neighbors, also divorced. The smile is involuntary. Born of fear. The way you smile at false authorities. (At the President.) Because I know that when I open the door, the cat will meet me with his eyes fixed on the damp doormat. Someday . . . I'll smack him in the nose. With the door. On purpose.

His latest stunt came when he turned eight months old and started demanding a mate. In a word, there's frequently a morning miracle at my house—an erection. At seven in the morning, while I'm drinking coffee, and the kid is still sleeping, do you know what the cat does? He climbs up on the zucchini Virga brought over and, straddling it with his powerful (Scots soccer player's) hind legs, he makes . . . the "movements of love." It wasn't long before the zucchini was all ragged and worn out. Do you think I'm going to eat it? (Do you think I'll ever eat another zucchini again?) Yes, the cat perches on it, purrs, and looks at me reproachfully. As if I was to blame for this, his . . . nature? Updike: "Sex part of nature before Christ."

Maybe that quote doesn't quite fit here. I've gone back through and counted eight quotations in this letter so far. Which probably means I've lost the ability to think independently. Or else I'm just overtired. I'm exhausted by the lingering insubstantiality of every-thing. Yes, criteria have vanished. Contexts have become confused. Sometimes I ask myself why I agreed to let the American make us a present of that cat in the first place. After all, I knew Goda wouldn't look after it: I was always going to be the one to change the litter, bathe it, and get up in the middle of the night to feed it. Then again, it seems to me that animals (as long as they're not clones) are the one real thing left in this world. Not simulacra. They don't know how to change themselves to suit the times or the market; they don't know how to put on an act. The media hasn't yet managed to manipulate them. For one thing, the bed on which my cat falls asleep the fastest is . . . a newspaper.

So, yesterday, castration day, dawned clear and sunny. I had made an appointment with the veterinarian a week before. I told Goda where I was going and let her go skating at the Akropolis shopping mall. The entire time, the cat sat calmly on the shelf next to some scattered pennies. The kid left. I called Potter when I was already dressed and kneeling next to his carrier. He obediently jumped down. When he jumped, his foot caught the money and one penny fell straight into his water bowl. I was really touched, because I knew why that had happened . . . When Goda came back from Saint Petersburg, she talked about what she'd seen . . . About the Orthodox churches with their gold turbans and the clouds made of feathers stuck behind them. About the drawbridges (which remind me of dentures, but I didn't say so). About a man going down an empty street in the morning, in the fog, with a real bear on a leash. My girl said, "Mama, I threw a kopeck in the fountain at Peterhof—will I really return to that place someday, like they say?" The cat heard this entire conversation. So that's why the poor thing decided, before his operation, to throw a penny into his bowl. So he'd return.

The animal clinic in the Old Town is better than the local one out in the suburbs. The veterinarian said, you've even been crying, but it's all going to be over within fifteen minutes, no more. There's already another patient waiting: a Doberman lying on a leather couch. They were going to clip the dog's ears, make them into ornaments. The gold chains on the dog and his master were identical. You know, if I had to live with a budding Mafioso like that dog's owner, I'd square off his pointy shoes with an axe, but make him wash out all that hair gel himself. The nurse asked, "Would you like to watch the operation?" I politely but immediately declined.

I went next door and drank two cups of coffee. Then I went back to the vet's office, dragging my feet, and saw the nurse standing in the door, waving to me—in other words, hurry up. That's it, I thought, he's dead. Couldn't take the anesthetic. In my hometown, a surgeon I know injected this rich guy's (also a Mafioso's) wife with spinal anesthesia. The woman died immediately, and the husband barged into the hospital with a gun and started off trying to shoot the cloakroom attendant. One in a million can't handle anesthesia, that's all, and it's impossible to test for it ahead of time. I approached the nurse; she led me to the operating table. The cat was lying there, dead center. Sleeping with his eyes wide open, his head turned in one direction, his tongue in the other. The doctor, all hot and sweaty, apologized:

"I won't charge anything for the anesthesia . . . it's my own fault. It didn't occur to me to examine him first. In seventeen years of practice it's the first time I've seen this pathology, even though it happens in people fairly often . . ."

"You mean his ears?" I asked (remembering the tactical question regularly posed to me by my Russian hairdresser at the Halė market: "Same as before? Shall we leave the ears open?")

"No, ma'am, I've seen dozens of Scottish Folds. Your cat has cryptorchidism. In layman's terms—he has no balls. His testicles haven't descended. Give me your hand . . . Do you feel it? Here, down deep. In his stomach. The other one, unfortunately, I can't find at all."

I groped the cat's velvety groin (with both hands) and started getting woozy. Roundish shapes began wandering around in my head—like small zucchinis, or giant florescent beads. I went out into the waiting room and collapsed next to the nervous Doberman in his muzzle. The nurse gave me valerian drops.

When I recovered, I asked what they thought I should do. The vet said that if even the cat's testicles aren't developed, it doesn't mean he won't want a mate. His brain still works, after all. He advised simply waiting. He warned me that if Potter started marking his territory, he'd need an operation anyway. And the operation would be difficult, worse than neutering a female. But if we don't operate, then he would be a prime candidate for testicular cancer. Because everyone's testicles—or, rather, all testicles—are meant to hang in the air. That is—outdoors. I mean, outside.

When I got home, I immediately called that guy who didn't go to the movies with me. I'm safe with him; I find him more comforting than anyone else. And I told him everything. He said: "You have to come to terms with it. Calm down. It makes sense, you know—if

anyone was going to fall at your feet, it *would* have be a cryptorchid."
Potter recovered toward evening: he threw up, but not much. He's
fine now. But last night I had a horrible dream. About divorce. My
dreams used to play many a variation on that subject. They'd stopped
long ago. In this dream, I was going to the Third Circuit Court to file
papers at my lawyer's. The corridors were dark and full of cobwebs,
and the walls wobbled when you leaned up against them—they gave
way like hammocks. So I was walking straight through room after
room, without using the doors. In one, my lawyer was sitting at a
desk. She was some eighty years old, but with serious cleavage. Her
breasts were plump, like a young woman's. She wore a pleated brown
wool skirt and Nike gym shoes. She pulled on rubber gloves, picked
up a ballpoint pen and a blank piece of paper, and asked:

"Spouse?"

"Scottish Fold," I say.

But she doesn't care for that at all: "Legally, neither your spouse's
nationality nor his looks are relevant. Unless he has ties to any nation-
alist terrorists in that region . . ."

"Not that I've noticed," I say. "In the seven months of . . . our
wedded life."

"Last name?"

"Potter."

Now the lawyer changed tacks and started trying to charm me,
and in a low voice, completely inappropriate to the situation, said,
"I bet I can guess his first name. Harry, right? 'Potter' has become a
really popular name around here. And, strangely enough, all of the
spouses who go by that name do indeed seem able to perform the
most amazing miracles. So: on what grounds, exactly, ma'am, do you
wish to divorce Mr. Potter?"

"Incompatibility, sex as part of nature, and . . . cryptorchidism."

The lawyer picked up a dusty little book, perhaps a Bible, opened
several already marked pages, saying regretfully, "According to the
civilian code, that's just not sufficient. There's no basis for a divorce.
Perhaps . . . he's having an affair?"

At that moment (in the dream) I start losing what's left of my grip
on reality. "He does," I say, "Hermione."

She brightens before my eyes, and almost instantly, the way they do in cartoons, writes up an entire page, on top of violet carbon paper, gives me one copy, and, taking her leave, informs me, "Every client is allowed three weeks to change their mind. You can cancel your claim until December 15."

I know what you're thinking. I made the dream up. It's too rational and logical. But did you know that Jean Baudrillard says that even dreams are manufactured now? I guess I've swallowed even that. All you have to do is guess who palmed it off on me, and why. Baudrillard also wrote that wherever we are, we live in a simulated universe that sometimes resembles the original, and that illusion has become impossible, because reality itself is impossible.

Listen, let's break with tradition this year. Come visit—not between the holidays, before New Year's, like you always do, but as soon as you can. You could come during the German Days festival in Vilnius. They're showing *The Blue Angel* with Marlene Dietrich. I could get you a ticket. The movie's supposedly about love, but what it's really about is how a man shouldn't change, not even for the woman he loves, because it will destroy him. Anyway, you do have the key to my apartment, after all.

But, look, when you come in, don't be surprised if you don't find anyone in the kitchen. The only thing that will greet you is a picture of Eminem on the refrigerator with his middle finger sticking out. Please go on to the middle room without delay and don't freak out—Potter has grown a lot. He started growing even before the visit to the veterinarian. I knew that cats usually start getting fat after a time, but generally only after they're fixed. As for me, I'm shrinking. Everyone gets smaller with age. Don't be afraid of snapping the mandarin tree's branches when you elbow your way into the living room. I brought the seed home with me from Chicago. Now it's grown so much I can't get it out of the room; last year the top even broke through the ceiling. My actor neighbor laughed when he told me about it. His son woke up in the morning (this is the boy I went to see *Karlsson* with) and stepped out of bed straight into the tip of the mandarin tree. He leaped back under the covers and said to his mother, "Let's not be afraid of anything. Like Freken Bok says, all sorts of things happen, even in the best of families." Anyway, shoulder your way through those branches, and if you break one or two, don't worry. The cat will be lying there, probably in the middle of the room, on the floor. Like a tiger under a tree. After everything I've told you, you'll probably understand that calling him "kitty, kitty" somehow doesn't seem appropriate. (Maybe you'd better not even pet him. Just go around.) I'll be sitting there too, leaning against his side, like the kid's Bratz doll (from the fall collection) is leaning against him now. I'll be reading a big book. I'll barely be able to hold it in my hands. And I'll give you one very important thought from that book, because I might forget to quote it later: "Technology is the knack of so arranging the world that we don't have to experience it." Then carefully pick me up and put me in Potter's carrier. Zip me up tight. (The more time passes, the more I'm afraid of the cold.) On the way out, take a thimble from my Italian jewelry box.

I'd like to go drink coffee with you in Pilies Street. If, when you pass the Aušros Gate, you turn back and stand there in thought a while, a piece of the wall's gold decoration might well fall at your feet. Take it: sometimes it brings luck. I'll want coffee with cream, by the way. In what used to be the Vaiva Café. We used to run over there for milk sausages in the breaks between classes. One time Linas, drunk, broke the corner of a lettuce-green cup. The waitress started yelling that she was tired of hooligans like him, and he threw himself over the bar, got right up into her face, and sang, *Marina . . .* Well, when you order coffee there, it'll all come back to you at once. (Because in the fall, time merges with space.) I'll drink my coffee in the carrier. Out of the thimble.

If, perchance, you can't come, then tomorrow I'll send you three things that have started irritating me in their obtuse opposition to reality. (You could take them to the cottage in Obeliai, or leave them at home, as you wish.) Don't get insulted. First, I'll send you a jar that's still a third full of honey. My mother gave it to me three years ago, when I was returning from Panevėžys to Vilnius. It's been two years already since she died. But the honey never seems to end. Of course, I don't use it much, really, just in the evenings for tea. But, anyhow . . . Next, you'll get an artificial silk scarf. There's a reproduction of a Renoir painting on it, a mother and daughter; I've forgotten what the painting's called. Don't bother tying it. Even a seaman's knot. It unties itself. I've lost it on hedges, the trolleybus, the streets.

If you do wear it, pin it on with something. Though the faces on it are so bright that you'll notice right away if it's fallen off your neck; you'll turn around and see them at once. And then, the last thing I'll send is a little wooden hand-cranked coffee mill with a little drawer. I bought it in an antique store in Chicago, on 47th Street. I returned to Lithuania five years ago. I've ground coffee in it many times. But the coffee always smells of some indeterminate spices, ground in that mill in some house in that city. I wonder if the population of Chicago has reached six million yet?

Good-bye! Kisses! (When I have e-mail again, I'll write a few sentences about how I'm getting along.) I always feel like you're close by. Like a watermelon seed in the stomach. Like cryptorchidism in the mouth. Jesus, I mean the other way around—like a watermelon seed in the mouth, like cryptorchidism in the stomach.

yr. g.

P.S. I mentioned the neighbor's dog. He's not a Tyzenschnauzer. I made a mistake. The breed is called a Riesenschnauzer. (Although, to me, when I love someone, neither their breed nor their looks are important.)

A Long Walk on a Short Pier

Some three months after the appearance of my first book, a well-known publisher I knew only by sight called me late in the evening. I don't like late calls. They have long been associated with family illnesses and my mother's friends checking to see if I'm doing anything illegal, for example, if I'm drinking wine in the kitchen with Nabokov again. "I'm disturbing you on account of the novel you're writing," the publisher said. "We'd like to read it." I assured him I wasn't writing anything. But it immediately became clear that he was going to patiently persevere. I told him he'd caught me during a reading phase. I write from experience—I can only write down as much as I live. I can no more write faster than live faster. Others construct reality—for money, with ease, and all the time. I don't even know how to make decent soup all the time, never mind fiction.

Besides, I had just then started on redecorating my apartment. Bought myself some putty. Some fabric. I'd been expecting an upholsterer for a couple of days already. He was supposed to cover a Klaipėda armchair, the Lithuanian equivalent of a La-Z-Boy, with Japanese hieroglyphics. When the publisher called, I was sitting on the floor, on top of the material I'd purchased, browsing through *Stilius* magazine. I was turning the pages and wondering how high-class women with nails like that manage to wipe their asses without hurting themselves. After a short pause, the publisher said, "But you *wrote* that you're writing. And in that one essay, you very insightfully—although, frankly, I think you needn't have been so sarcastic about it—listed everything that a best-selling novel needs: exotica, complaints about God, sex of a somewhat unusual . . ." "Sure," I interrupted him, "and in another essay, I wrote that a girlfriend took me downtown in a cat carrier to have a cup of coffee, and that her father finds women most useful for pulling ticks out of his back." Whenever I get interrupted, I lose all desire to converse further, but this man, in the nearly indifferent voice of an experienced gambler, pressed on: "Well, yes, it's difficult to tell fiction from reality. Just because you have a gentle narrator doesn't mean its author isn't merciless in real life. But look, one way or the other, I'm sure that you'll write a novel sooner or later, as there are perfectly viable longer narratives—buried, but still alive and kicking—running through parts of your various essays. I'll call, if I may, about every four months. Think about it carefully. I'm sure you've heard it before, but what is a writer these days without a novel under her belt? A nobody. In other words—nothing but a columnist. If you aren't on the cover of a novel, you're nowhere. Strange as it may seem, the best-seller lists are still dominated by novels, you know. Sometimes I wonder why, myself. You know, a person comes home, sinks into an armchair, and wants to be launched into outer space for a while . . . that's what stories are for, they take you out of yourself. The reader wants to leave life behind, become indeterminate, neither here nor there. To disconnect himself. To become a detective, or a murderer. Do a little traveling. Find true love, feel lots of exciting emotions. In short, to make a clean getaway from one's own boring skin. When I was little I used to read *The Three Musketeers* that way, but I still had to do my homework, so as soon as I read a paragraph of chemistry or physics I'd reward myself with Dumas for a half-hour. Now I see my daughter reading *There's a Boy in the Girls' Bathroom* the same way. Short stories don't cut it—they don't last long enough to really get into them. There's none of the allure of the long journey. You know, it's like floating in a rowboat, just drifting, pleasantly, with the shore far away, but not dangerously so. Of course, a novel still has to end before it begins to feel like a burden, an obligation. Five-hundred-page books use up their credit very quickly. Unless the narrative is propped up by some kind of quest, or investigation. Henning Mankell, Unni Lindell, John Irving, Haruki Murakami, Dan Brown . . . I say the mystery novel is the basic form to which we should all aspire. Not literally, of course. When I say 'investigation,' I don't necessarily mean a whodunit. Why not a quest for one's sexual identity, for example? In one of your essays you wrote that you felt as though you'd lost your gender. A great beginning for a novel . . . or end for a life. No, no, I'm kidding. But you're mistaken when you say, as you did in the title of one of your essays, that the plot should be shot dead. The celebrated essay genre is basically a parasite, right from the start, thriving at the expense of real literature. All that topicality, the irrepressible exhibitionism of our essayists, well, the river of time drowns them soon enough. Writers think they're talking about solitude, for example, when they're actually just fondling their wilting genitalia. Yes, yes, it's as difficult to squeeze existentialism out of that particular spot as it is to squeeze sweat from a stone. Sex . . . Well, you probably remember what that art historian said: Sex is like eating plums. And eroticism is like smelling flowers. But where's love in all that? When human feelings have been impoverished to the point where they're nothing more than mechanical movements, they can only be of interest to soldiers. And I mean the old-timers, not the new recruits. I think sex without love really is like eating plums. That is, with a big pit in the way. But, look, with writing, the most important thing is not to be afraid to start. Do you know what Bernard Shaw said to a lady who asked him how he wrote? He said, from left to right. Perhaps the problem is that you're intimidated by the so-called seriousness of the novel genre? The weight of it all? Plots, central conflicts, character development, endings reflecting important social realities . . . What silliness. This isn't the era of Anna Karenina. Just make up your mind; your train will surely arrive. Essentially any text, you know, even a novel, is just a bunch of free-floating thoughts written down. Although it would be ideal if they were interspersed with recipes, if that's not too much to ask. Not that that hasn't already been done. But, you know, on the way to the Baltic, Esquivel's water for chocolate and Allende's aphrodisiacs all turned into mushrooms—mushrooms, mushrooms, and more mushrooms. In Lithuania women even make their salads according to Laima Muktupavela's memoir *The Mushroom Covenant*. So there's still room to sprout, I say. A novel can be about anything. Getting started is what's most important. Oh, and the ability to end the thing in good time. Like I said, before reading becomes an obligation. Are you still there? Hello? Am I interrupting something? What are you thinking? Whatever it is, I'm certain it could turn into the first sentence of your novel . . . Just so long as it isn't one of those five-page sentences . . ."

I'll tell you what I was thinking. I was thinking that probably in the twelfth century or earlier, before the mechanical clock had been invented, women preparing food would measure the time for cooking a dish by the number of psalms they read. I'd want someone reading my work to burn their beans to cinders.

Although I naturally enjoy disputing any sort of strict rule, it's still clear to me that the first sentence of any text really is extremely important. It shouldn't begin with a participle or a gerund, because instead of fine-tuning the fundamental action they only weaken it. It's imperative to avoid too "poetic" a diction—no "halt"s or "nay"s, please. They make living language reek of the tomb; no matter how witty your metaphors, you can't shake off that smell afterward. And while interjections might appear to be one of the most meaningless parts of speech at first glance, in reality they're a powerful tool. One of an acquaintance's school friends, who stayed behind in the country to raise four kids, wrote him a letter inviting him to come visit in the summer with his own family. She ended the letter intending to make humorous use of the interjection "ahem"—never used casually, and generally reserved, in print, for snide reviews. Her mind must have wandered, however, as it came out like this: "On the solstice, my brother will be coming too, with his kids; we'll build a bonfire, and everyone can go have a dip in the lake. If you're not coming— amen!—be sure to let me know."

Despite everything, the publisher had sown a seed in my brain. He had thrown an offer at my feet like one of Dumas's heroes might throw down his glove. Did I really not have it in me to write a book? A real one. Some three hundred pages. Two hundred fifty, at the very least. Pamela Anderson managed it. Madonna. Even her little daughter is writing now, I hear. (Mama's editing it.) I've long since known that just about any nonsense, written down with some basic understanding of grammar, can become a book in most people's eyes. It's not the text that's important; it's the image. What a trap. As Camus said: "Any artist who goes in for being famous in our society must know that it is not he who will become famous, but someone else under his name, someone who will eventually escape him and perhaps someday will kill the true artist in him."

In order for a writer to make herself an "image," I think, one needs to begin with three things—a face, a name, and a lifestyle. When I mentioned to my neighbor that I wanted to get braces put on my teeth because I wanted to have my picture taken, and thought I should look up-to-date for the occasion, he asked me how much they would cost. And that was the right question. Money is my weak spot. For example, I only find rich men handsome. To me, their attractiveness is directly dependent on their bank accounts. Back when I used to see a psychiatrist, she said this was an instinct typical of both sexes (but more, perhaps, of women), and even as I got older and, let's say, wiser, I would never really be able to entirely overcome that flaw. Supposedly, she added, when the economy is in an upswing, it helps suppress this instinct a bit. My neighbor advised me, in the end, against donating thousands to my dentist. Rather than braces, he said, just have your picture taken with the teeth of a zipper stuck under your upper lip.

Still, even when money is involved, a woman like me would only ever agree to change her name through a unique convergence of coincidence and sentiment. And I, a forty-five-year-old woman, being of completely sound mind and of my own free will, as they say, have sent love packing. But, two weeks ago, purely by chance, I started getting letters from an aging American man. He got my address from a distant relative of mine. He was searching for an "intelligent woman who has a sense of humor" to be his pen pal. I liked his last name best—Faulkner. Oh, and his parrots. He sent me pictures of them, and himself, via e-mail. One of the birds knows how to say "Hannah wants a cracker." And why not have a different last name, after all? Giedra Faulkner . . .

In the evenings, it's quiet now at my and my daughter's building. Sometimes it seems as if the quiet is flowing from me like oil. I hear my houseplant shooting its ripened seeds at the window from a swollen, three-sided pod. I close my eyes, freeze, "And suddenly, like in the ads, Eternity. But not the time. Not the place." The cat and I take turns sipping tea with milk from an English porcelain saucer.

Later we bite our nails. It's a habit I seem to have picked up recently. I blame reality shows. I watch them too often. I bite my nails because I'm afraid. Because it seems to me that the people on those shows, on their first days—I mean the people as they once were, when they arrived at a studio for the first time—"disappear without a trace," and no one even notices. Whereas the cat bites his nails because he doesn't like it when I cut them with special scissors—something I can only do after first pretending—despicably—that I'm only coming over because I want to pet him. Later I find his clippings in my slippers or the breadbox. And sometimes we share an armchair and listen to salsa. If his tail should drop off the edge of the chair, the cat quickly nudges it back with his paw; it offends him that not all of him can fit on the cushion at once. The salsa CD was left for me at a certain publisher's by an unknown person who added an unaggressive little love letter. Signed it "Johnsiera." When I asked what the man who brought the disc looked like, the women in the office shrugged their shoulders, as if he'd been November's wind or snow. I like the frothy rhythm of salsa—it too is like November's wind and snow . . . And I happen to think that "Johnsiera" is not a he but a she, a friend of mine who translates Polish poetry for that publisher—but I haven't said anything to her yet. Let her believe she's pulled the trick off.

When the trains go by at night, I hear my room's doors and windows vibrating. Like an earthquake building to a crescendo. This summer, after the earthquake we had in Vilnius, a Danish tourist was given the following instructions: when you feel the first vibrations, stand in a doorway holding some kind of identification. The doorway provides some protection from objects (or plaster) falling from above, while the documents come in handy when it comes time to identify what's left of you. When the ground starting shaking again a few hours later, he took up his post in the doorway of the Čili pizzeria—both hands clutching whatever personal documents he'd brought along, and with a Vilnius bank card between his teeth.

In the bathtub, having a long soak, I sometimes hear a dog barking. A big, vicious, energetic one, and not old yet, either. I sink underwater to get away from the sound. How often I've tried, most meticulously, to deduce who lives to the left of me. I know the seamstress Liuda only has a female cat. When the cat went into heat (on the 14th of February—as though she'd planned it), the thing pooped on my doormat. Out of anger and desire (they're frequently related), because she smelled my own cat, but he, no matter how she meows, refuses to answer. Like me, he doesn't like flirting through doors. Downstairs on the left is a fried meat pie cafe, and the neighbors above me have only children. So there's nothing beyond the thick bathroom wall, the way I figure it. Except for another building, which, when you're looking at it from outside, seems like part of the same building. There could be a small closed courtyard, too. I imagine it overgrown with chickweed; perhaps there's a pump in the center, painted with oils. But I've never come across anyone coming out of the other gateway with a dog. For four years now, that barking while I'm bathing has been a hairy mystery to me. One of Cortázar's characters had a similar problem. His was the sound of a woman's resigned weeping all night long in a hotel room. He was tormented by it, or rather from speculating as to what could cause such inexhaustible weeping. The man nearly went insane from lack of sleep. But afterward, it seems, some kind of story developed out of it.

Changing your name, or changing your face, is easy compared with changing your lifestyle. But I've made up my mind. The same way I always have to force myself to go to the dentist after a long interval. One quiet evening, I approached my daughter as she was doing her homework. Before beginning this difficult—and time-consuming, as I anticipated initially—conversation, I twice tried to fix the creased carpet with my foot, pushing both her slippers tidily into their spot. My daughter was facing away from me, doing a geography assignment, reading about the glaciers that once slid over Europe and so altered the continent's landscape forever.

"My child," I said, "I have something important to tell you. I got a phone call from a very wise publisher, you know. He suggested I write a novel. For money. I've decided to take his advice and become a real writer. I'm going out . . . I have to think it all through. Perhaps we'll have to change the way we live. Hitch our banal existence to eternity. Just like the dead."

"I have a test tomorrow," she replied. "If you go by the supermarket, bring back some wafers. Two packages. The chocolate ones, please." Without even turning around.

I put a spare pair of panty hose, a bottle of valerian extract, some brandy, a small volume of Nabokov, and my daughter's photograph into a canvas bag bearing the slogan "Don't Leave Home Without It." Then I put on my coat in the hallway. Opening the door to the frosty Old Town—put into perfect order by our new mayor, but still full of surprises—I find myself telling myself that I am absolutely doing the right thing. That my mother, who died three years ago and in whose coffin I put a sprig of jasmine while no one was looking, would forgive me.

My eighth-grader was surely too young to understand that if you want to become a real writer, you leave home for good. You begin to shape your life, like Jurgis Kunčinas would say, "from the start." Writers are damned. The truly talented and passionate ones abandon their children entirely. To wives and husbands. Sisters and brothers. Fate and the law. Writers follow the rhythm of their hearts; they live apart, humming with everyday life despite keeping their eyes on eternity. In order to protect his or her talent, in order to go on providing so much happiness to thousands of very likely unhappy people, a writer cannot have either a house, or a job, or money, or any sort of peace, spiritually speaking. He must be steeped in loneliness. Must torture himself. Drink a lot, and starve a lot . . . At this point, the rhythm of my heart, without my even remembering to consult it, testified that I was on the right path. Invention must be the writer's daily and only bread. The plowed fields of inspiration, watered by our bloody sweat, where tender crocuses open . . . (Semantically speaking, perhaps "delicate" would have been a better adjective than "tender.") Exotica. Complaints about God. Eternity. The dead. Image after image. And . . . how did he put it? Interspersed with recipes. The novelist must listen for whom the bell tolls, and climb the magic mountain. Wander from here to eternity, across the river and into the trees. Like Homo Faber, the invisible man, or the mighty angel. I turn around . . . On the second floor, light leaks through the linen curtains, out here into the heart of darkness. Bring home some wafers. Two packages . . . chocolate. Ahead: the city and the dogs. Or do I mean the time of the hero. Light in August, anyway. One hundred years of solitude. Immortality. Feeling the tears brimming up in my eyes, I'm gone with the wind . . . Yes, blown from here to eternity. Look homeward, angel. But it's not for those who have left to return.

It gets dark. The Old Town, perhaps because of all its lights, gets dark more slowly than out beyond the railroad tracks. Out there lives a jeweler who once made me a silver ring with an alexandrite stone. The sky this night was exactly that color—purple with pink edges. And the evening was like the one after my divorce when I smashed the wedding crockery painted with forget-me-nots. I went out that night dressed in a jogging suit, with a cardboard box under my arm, and battered six cups and a coffee pot on the railroad ties. Back then, the big trees next to the railroad tracks hadn't been cut down yet. When I took out the garbage, bats would fly over my head like rocks from a slingshot.

In the dusk, the thought came to me that a person isn't aged by years but by perceptions. I should start my novel with an episode in paradise. The narrator will be dead, but it should seem to the readers that the woman is only relaxing in a small resort town. A long walk on a short pier is on the agenda, as the cynical English would say. Because I'm a pessimist. I'm always gathering up the worst impressions from my past and out of them cobbling together a future just as grim. Nabokov said about novels: "It's queer, I seem to remember my future works, although I don't even know what they will be about. I'll recall them completely and write them down." Nowadays, when you bring a manuscript to your publisher you can suggest a design for the cover at the same time. And I'll give the book an ordinary sort of title: *In Those Days, When I was Alive*. Here's a shot at it:

"While resting, my thoughts often returned to the past. Sometimes, for no apparent reason, the wind would suddenly come up and carry slight swirls of sand along the streets. They reminded me of the silhouette of the genie escaped from his bottle in a book of old fairy tales I read as a child. On the far bank, little bells never stopped ringing, seemingly unconnected to the wind. I would imagine that they were hanging in clusters from the necks of camels, although more likely they decorated some goat or cow. By the way, I also noticed the smell of manure. I somehow never thought that even here, so close to God, domestic animals would be grazing freely and houses would be built according to some kind of social hierarchy as well. Sand, berries, and clouds resembling stuffed toys. It was impossible to reconcile the notion of camels— wandering in from a photo in some Turkish tourist brochure ('Marmaris . . . We all deserve paradise at least once in our lives')—with the blackberries ripening next to that stone cottage. An impossible combination, like the lions and birch trees in Wiiralt's etchings. Standing a while by the river, one would inevitably see household goods floating by—a striped mattress, for example, and bits of wood from rotten doorjambs. It was difficult to believe that a modern black bus (if of uncertain manufacture) brought me to those mountains. When we were leaving, the director warned us to under no circumstances offer the driver money. Even though it was unlikely that the elderly people who'd spent the night on the bus had any. Aside from one or another anniversary coin, perhaps. As soon as I got on the bus, we were gliding down the mountain road without a sound, and I remembered an advertisement for a luxury car. Above there was a gold BMW; below, in letters as red as blood: 'In a car like this, the only thing that clatters is your wife's teeth.'"

So far, in this text, what I like most is the ambiguity about that "director," which makes the reader wonder, is this a movie, a tour, or a funeral . . . ? Next to the horrible intersection by the Aušros Gate, I stopped to wait for the green light. Across from me was a billboard with a picture of a couple of kids drawn with mushroom caps on their heads: "They sprout out of nowhere. Drivers, beware!" I stepped back from the road a bit. Because my aunt had just recently told me about two incidents that had stuck in her mind all her life: One of them was the death of a child, the other the deaths of two women. Happily, my healthy instinct for self-preservation had already managed to erase all the details of the child's death from my memory, but regarding the two women, it all happened in the sixth decade of the last century. They were walking just here, in the spot where I stand now. My aunt was behind them on her way to the Pedagogical Institute. She was studying German and Spanish, at the time. In Spanish, the word "to live" in the second person plural is *vivís*. But, in Spanish, *v* is pronounced like *b*, so the word comes out sounding like the word for "penis" in Lithuanian. Well, my aunt and one of her friends just couldn't keep from laughing when their elegant lecturer, wearing a snood on her hair, and so very much in love with the doomed heroes of the Spanish Civil War, would say *bybys* as she conjugated the verb, and on that day they were even expelled from the lecture hall for it. So, the two women walking in front of my aunt wanted to cross to the other side of the street, but at that moment a truck suddenly turned from one side of the Aušros Gate toward the railroad station. It was carrying thick plates of glass. During the sharp turn, some of the plates of glass that were strapped to its side peeled off and cut the women on the sidewalk to pieces. After that, the word *vivís* had a completely different meaning for my aunt. She said that it became as familiar to her as her raincoat. And even a bit Lithuanian. And my uncle, hearing this story, commented, "Well, didn't you know that God is on the other side of the Gate of Dawn?"

On the other side of the Aušros Gate, a good deal lower down, there was once a cafeteria where my mother did an internship while she was studying at the Technical School of Commerce. It's not there anymore, but you can walk by the spot. In the cafeteria it smelled of ordinary vegetables—boiled potatoes, beets, carrots—and aluminum pots clattered there all day long. One hot spring, the old cook, Mirikas, who'd been assigned to the girls, taught them how to make real lemonade. You need only six lemons in all. Plus sugar and water. You peel the skins off of three lemon halves and cook a syrup out of them with sugar. Then you mix this with the juice squeezed out of the remaining lemons and dilute it a bit more with boiled water. You must drink it with ice. (Preferably crushed.) The glass may be decorated with lemon slices. (Real orangeade, as far as I know, is boiled out of bitter oranges as well as lemon. And is diluted with rose water, which we never had, and still don't.) I suppose it's only really in the novels of Southern authors from the US that one can buy lemonade like that from little wagons on the side of the road—Eudora Welty's fiction, for example (and maybe Faulkner's). But Mirikas taught the girls many other food-preparation tricks as well. Unbelievably simple, many of them. For example, if you want your soup to be thick, you shouldn't slice the potatoes, but boil them whole and then break them into pieces with a knife or fork. For the rest of her life, Mama would only sprinkle in her spices at a certain moment, a few minutes before the cooking was finished, and she never covered the pot afterward.

The girls working at the cafeteria, since they didn't have much else to do, took up teasing Mirikas a bit. Mama started calling him from a telephone booth almost every day, during the lunch break. She'd talk with a handkerchief over the receiver. "I've been watching you for almost a year now. Today you went to work looking sad again. I eat lunch at the cafeteria and I see you through the kitchen door, always surrounded by beautiful women." The idea was to make it seem as though a stranger had fallen in love with him, someone who worked nearby, maybe even across the street—someone who was too shy to approach him directly.

Mirikas got a haircut. Started going to work wearing a different plaid shirt every day. On his way, he would look into the shop windows, then still rare in that area. The girls brought a record player to the cafeteria kitchen so it'd be even more cheerful, and constantly listened to a song whose refrain was "Ding, dong, don't be wrong . . ." My mother, "in character," arranged to meet Mirikas in the plaza at the Art Museum, purposely picking a place where anyone would be visible from a good distance away. Mirikas waited for his secret admirer for an hour. The girls were congregated on a bench, watching. They ate three servings of ice cream each, but didn't approach him. And thereafter stopped calling. Now Mirikas began showing his age, all at once; he even became gaunt. He orchestrated all the food prep sitting down, whereas earlier he'd run around the kitchen with the bottom edges of his long white coat stuck in his pockets to keep them from flapping around. A few months later, the old man died. By then, Mama was working in a restaurant in the town where I would be born. A friend from school called and said there was a rumor going around Vilnius that the old man had hanged himself. The public story was that he'd died from complications related to the flu, but various details contradicting this circulated among the girls: Supposedly, a lacquered metal box decorated with rye fields and Russian troikas had disappeared from Mirikas's locked room. A nephew apparently had intentions on his apartment. When the old man died, an anonymous person called the police immediately. Actually, on the last day of my mother's internship, Mirikas had arranged a farewell party for the girls. He made beef stroganoff and lemonade. He invited Mama into the cloakroom and presented her with an antique engraved metal teapot without a lid. Her friends said it was because she was the prettiest of the group, but I know Mama thought otherwise. (I wouldn't be at all surprised if the nephew had found a record of that "Ding, dong" song in Mirikas's room after he died . . .)

I was now standing in Didžiosios Street, only as far the Rimi supermarket. All these memories—or maybe it was the brandy—had dried my mouth out. How had I managed to finish off the brandy I'd brought along, just between the railroad and here? I kept taking sips from the little bottle, keeping it pressed inside my "Don't Leave

Home Without It" bag. I remembered the cat was out of kitty litter. And the kid had asked for wafers. (Two packages. Chocolate.) There was nothing but foreigners in the store, going downstairs into the basement. Perhaps some event was going on? When Mama was a student, the Moscow movie theatre had stood here. Later it was renamed the Helios. Next, I'm sure there will be a beachhead of the Armani empire here. The interior in nothing but black and white. With orchids. (Likewise white.)

I inevitably turn into a klutz in big stores. In the vegetable section, I lost my scarf. And then, I sat down on the plastic carriers stacked up next to the front door and pulled up my skirt; I needed to shake a pebble out of my shoe. The pebble fell out, but the run in my stocking was already all the way up to the back of my knee. I pulled the extra pantyhose out of my bag. I moved my face up close to the mirrored wall, so close that the sweat on the tip of my nose left a mark. I felt that I looked terrible and needed to touch up my makeup a bit. I didn't know that the mirrored wall was two-way. Just like in police movies. A mirrored door opened up and a security guard appeared. He was looking right at me: I imagined the crime blotter in the next day's paper—"Confronted by the officer, there was a verbal altercation, followed by a physical one."

Rattling keys between his fingers, the guard asked, "Madam, you're waiting for someone?" "I'm waiting," I answered, "For a stroke, like my brother had. And diabetes—like my sister." And I thought, if they want to take the kid away from me, I'll fight them tooth and claw. But he just sent me on my way. Stumbling at nearly every step, I headed out of the supermarket back to the street. It was almost dark. Even though the Old Town gets dark more slowly than over there, past the railroad tracks. A young woman without a foot asked for money. I didn't give her anything. At the newspaper stand a slightly crumpled *Stern* magazine featured an interview with Elfriede Jelinek. That was the first time I saw her in furs. In the dark, that new material they put on the sidewalks, galvaniced steel, looked really slick, but it was just a little wet. Before he retired, my grandfather worked in a galvanizing shop at a factory. He would lower heavy parts into huge, stinking pots coated in green slime, covering them with a new layer of metal. Sometimes he'd bring in Grandmother's worn-out knives and forks. After a few years the utensils would start peeling again, like chocolate-wrapper foil.

"You're the one who always tells me not to forget the keys, so I can unlock the door myself," my daughter said as she opened the door for me. "The upholsterer hasn't covered the chair yet," she continued. "He was here, but he left again. For cigarettes. Oh, and Rūta called, and *Books from Lithuania*, and then some woman."

I felt like I was going to puke at any moment, but I started making some soup for the upholsterer. That was part of the deal—while he was working, there would be soup. His eighteen-year-old son had multiple sclerosis. He was already bedridden, but the process, thank God, was moving very slowly. Every day, on his way home from work, the upholsterer would rent a couple of thrillers for his son at the Old Town video store. We can all understand the urge to spoil a sick child. I saw something similar in Chicago. The yearly military air show was going on. The newest fighter jets were flying over Lake Michigan. First the plane would appear, and only when it disappeared again over the horizon would you hear the sound. The pilots took their jets down to only a few hundred feet above the water, and the lake would hollow out in a shining ring around them. Next to me, on the street, amid thousands of people, sat a boy in a wheelchair. An IV was attached to his arm. His parents had brought him there. The boy's face was the same color as the sand. But his eyes, watching the airplanes, were happy.

(Now: ideally, the following conversation between the narrator and her daughter would be presented like a dream. But dreams only crop up in lyrical prose, and I'm writing an essay.)

"'Some woman'? What woman?" I asked.

"She only spoke up after I said hello three times. And she said, don't be afraid, it's me calling, your grandmother. I see you and your mother every day from here, where I'm at now, but I really wanted to hear your voice, my dear. Please don't hang up, we only get one phone call here. They give you an extra two minutes if you bring some object along with you. I gave them a dried-up sprig of jasmine."

My daughter's never lied to me. Or, anyway, I've never caught her in a lie. But feeling like I did, about to throw up, I hurried into the bathroom and started running the hot water. I put my hand under the tap. The kid followed me and stood in the doorway.

"So I said to her, all right, if you're my grandmother who died three years ago and you see us all the time, then tell me what my mother's bringing home for me? From the supermarket."

Being of sound mind, as they say, I simply kept quiet. I watched my face slowly disappear in the bathroom mirror as steam fogged it over. I knew I that should "let it go." But what if . . . ? Whoever or whatever the creature who called was, she had to realize she couldn't tell my daughter I was bringing home chocolate wafers. Because then my daughter would have (as I did once) drunk magic water from the footprint of a lamb and turned into something she couldn't put a name to for the rest of her life.

"Did she guess?" I asked, standing naked now in front of the mirror, which was blank as a wall.

"Mom, sometimes you're as dumb as the cat. Of course not. She just asked me to recite a poem instead. I got mad. I told her to take a hike. We'll upholster the furniture, Mama will bring me home some wafers, and you could be anyone—there's no such thing as heaven . . . I heard this noise on the line, you know, a grating sound, like when they're sandblasting a building. Then she said, I won't call again. Your mother will surely come home soon. Say hello to her for me. And tell her . . . when she makes soup, don't slice the potatoes. For the soup to be thick, she needs to break them into rough pieces."

When I next emerged from under my bathwater, the kid was no longer there. Even though I still felt like I was going to vomit, I thought I might be able to get to sleep. In any case, I told myself, the next day, sobered up, I would feel considerably better. I would go to the market first thing in the morning to buy some fresh beef. Saturday. Perhaps the upholsterer would even finish covering the armchair. Every piece of furniture, they say in the ads, has an intimate purpose too. And there's more caramel and peanuts in chocolate bars these days. When you order new glasses, you can get the frames for free. Things aren't entirely bleak. And, yesterday the woman's magazine *Stilius* came out. There was a quiz in last week's issue that was supposed to tell you how passionate you are. One of the things confirming this, in my case, was my yes to the question, "Have you ever read a novel you liked in one sitting?" And something else I particularly appreciated reading is that Colombard grapes in France are still picked by hand. This, precisely, is how a noble drink is born, with its rich aromas of flowers, honey, tobacco, and chocolate . . . Cognac (like brandy) should be made in the same way it should be enjoyed—slowly and leisurely . . .

Slowly and leisurely, I pulled the plug out of the bathtub, because I realized I was about to fall asleep there and then. The water even roared as it gushed into the drain—Slavka changed the pipes recently, a year ago. I stood up, grabbed a towel . . . And suddenly, as usual unexpectedly, beyond the thick wall, on the left, a dog started barking. A large, energetic, and not yet old one.

Even though I was sick of it, as I dried off in front of the slowly recovering mirror I once again meticulously considered who might live to the left of me. I know the seamstress Liuda has a cat. Below, there's a fried meat pie cafe. Above, the neighbors only have children. For four years now that barking dog has been a hairy mystery to me. The riddle faced by one of Cortázar's characters was the resigned weeping of a woman all night long in a hotel room. He was tormented by it, or rather from speculating as to what could cause it. The man nearly went insane from lack of sleep. But afterward some kind of story developed out of it.

My American Biography

In 1960, the year I was born in a provincial town, Soviet soldiers shot down the American U-2 spy plane piloted by Francis Gary Powers, which had been investigating all our great USSR's private parts, so to speak. In the newspaper *Tiesa,* someone drew black hawks wearing American military hats perched on top of the Statue of Liberty. They held bombs in their claws. Mama, like all the other women in town, thought that this event was going to be the beginning of war with America. The month of May was nearly over, the best time for the five-year plan's required sowing of all our imported American corn, and everyone was weighing Khrushchev's statements to de Gaulle, Macmillan, and Eisenhower. All of life's little discomforts faded in the light of our expectations of catastrophe. No one paid the least attention to the mess at home; it even passed unnoticed that they'd brought me home from the birthing center with lice. Although the Soviet leaders claimed they would not sit down at the meeting table with aggressors, they apparently seated themselves there anyway, as they later exchanged Powers for some colleague of their own. Ordinary people don't know how exchanges like that happen, but I imagine them like the scene in the 1969 Russian movie *Dead Season.*

Father was still very good, then, and used to let my mother out to go to the movies. She wasn't particularly crazy about the movies themselves, but apparently she sometimes longed for distant countries and fancy clothes—in a word, a different atmosphere. Mama worked in the station restaurant's kitchen. She never put on a hat on her way home, even in winter, so that by the time she got back the smell of sunflower oil—from the donuts cooked there every day—would be out of her hair. One Sunday, coming home from *The Great Caruso*, she tripped over a bit of uneven sidewalk on the main street, fell down, and broke her arm. In the hospital, it became clear that the arm would have to be operated on because it was an open fracture. When I hear "open fracture," I imagine a St. Petersburg bridge raised at night. I wish medical terms were even less straightforward than they already are. Anyway, when the doctor found out that there was a three-month-old baby at home, he immediately examined Mama's breasts, saying, "With so little milk, we'll never catch up with America anyway." ("We" who?) So Mama stayed in the hospital, and gave me to my grandparents, to raise in an even smaller town.

When I was already bigger than the poppies growing in the garden by the house and no longer sucking on a pacifier, I took note of the people going by in the yard, the so-called neighbors. Russian military officers, settled there by the Soviet government, lived on the top floor of our building. A court had ruled that Grandfather purchased the house unlawfully, because its previous owner had forged the title to the property. I have all the documents from the case to this day. Sometimes I like to run my finger over the yellowed blueprints to the building, to remember the corridors in that house, and to find the small room in which I used to imagine being menaced by a bearded dwarf; I remember that a salt barrel eaten by rust used to stand just there. In those years, several similar cases were heard in town, during which those participating in the lawsuit, some of them armed with revolvers, were living in the same house. My grandfather couldn't talk about the lawsuit without trembling in anger, but nonetheless he'd sometimes go and drink a bottle of moonshine with those officers in our sitting room. They called my grandfather *batya*, Dad, entirely innocently, while he, as soon as evening fell, would come into our rooms and turn on the radio to listen to the news, which always began with the sentence, "This is the Voice of America, speaking to Lithuania from Europe." I didn't understand why Grandmother would immediately cover the windows, close the shutters, and tell me to talk in a whisper. The radio didn't seem to be saying anything special. The pleasant voices of men and women kept on talking about the important meetings Kennedy had attended, and his worries over Ecuador. Kennedy would say over and again that America's relationship with the Soviet Union was important not just to his country, but to the entire world. Without understanding anything, just watching the blinking green eye of the radio, I'd listen to the news, and later I used to imagine that the Statue of Liberty had eyes that flashed in just the same way.

On Fridays, Grandfather would bathe. After his sauna, he would cut the hairs sticking out of his nose, then cut the calluses off of his heels with a pocketknife, and throw them into a drawer. Then he would put on the clean pair of underwear thrown over the chair ahead of time, and sit down to eat some milk soup. When he caught the spot of melting butter with his spoon, he would sigh out his content in one word: "*Amerika* . . ." Looking at that spot of butter, I began to understand that in America things were the way they ought to be in this world—clean, bountiful, and just. Not like they were in our house, where heel calluses rattled around our drawers and men with revolvers lived over our heads.

"Where is America?' I asked my grandfather once, wanting to understand his sigh of bliss.

"There." Spooning soup with his right hand, he pointed at the floor with his left forefinger, apparently having the other side of the earth in mind. Perhaps because his finger had been cut once and had healed with a squared-off tip, the location of America remained a mystery to me. Right up until he died. Grandfather almost seemed to enjoy having taken this secret with him into his coffin—where he lay dressed in a blindingly white shirt sent to him from America by a cousin who had emigrated.

When, eventually, I was sent to school, and we were studying the continent of North America, which I thought resembled a rooster hung up by its feet, I remembered Grandfather's forefinger pointing at the floor. That finger, breaking the crust of the earth, penetrating its many layers to emerge on the Atlantic shore with its nail full of Miami sand . . .

It was around then, I'm told, that father began leaving us. I say "began leaving" because only cynics leave their families all at once. Father was a true romantic: he wrote poems, collected herbariums, and even had tuberculosis. If he had decided to stick to poetry, perhaps everything would have turned out all right, but no, he had to take up writing prose. I'm convinced that people only throw themselves into writing prose when all other avenues have been closed to them—it's an act of desperation. And Father's one and only story was about his solitude, which was apparently expressible only through art. His main character, a lonely dreamer, observed ordinary life from a distance: "From his study window he can see the street. It is not far away, since the lawn is not deep. It is a small lawn, containing a half dozen lowgrowing maples. The house, the brown, unpainted and unobtrusive bungalow is small too and by bushing crepe myrtle and syringa and althea almost hidden save for that gap through which from the study window he watches the street." It's that althea which always makes me feel most sorry for my father. He, the herbarium collector, could so easily have swapped that swamp plant for something better. And an editor was already planning to print my father's story in the town newspaper, but he too noticed the althea, and, since he happened to be reading Faulkner's *Light in August* at the time, he recognized the sentences . . .

Right after that, father disappeared. For a month he was supposedly at a famous sanatorium—on account of his lungs—but then he returned to the house after all, just to get his books. Rushing (apparently he was afraid of running into Mama, coming home from work), he piled both Faulkner, whom he knew by heart, and all my fairy-tale books into his suitcase. I didn't so much enjoy reading those fairy-tale books as I liked looking through the little colored pictures. If no one was at home, I would even scare myself looking at them. The witch with orange hair and the dragon with three heads on its disgusting neck would seem to come to life. They would sneak away from their pages in the book and stand behind me, staring.

The next summer I went with my older cousin to an amusement park; we wanted to ride the Ferris wheel. When we got to the very highest point, where it always seems as though you're hanging in the air without support, instead of taking in the entire small town below us at a glance, I looked down and saw my father there, walking down a path with his second wife. And at that same moment, my car broke off the wheel, and slowly, softly, as though it were the down coverlet my grandmother had made for my mother rather than a piece of metal, it glided down right on top of the walking couple . . . For some time afterward, still feeling the desire of that fantasy, I would often dream that I was falling, but Mama would stroke my head and say that it wasn't anything to be afraid of. All children dream of falling; it means they're growing.

At school I differed from the other kids at the top of the class because I lacked both jeans and a father. I've already told you about Father; I was jeanless for several reasons. First, my mother didn't have the money to buy them; second, I don't like to see tight-fitting behinds, unless they're on a bicycle or a motorcycle. Not all of my classmates bought their jeans at the market; frequently, relatives from America would send them. They wore down those jeans down to the paleness of an enameled pot, after which they'd cut them into pieces and sell the strips to other kids as patches. Now Gvidas, he didn't have a father either, but he did wear jeans. He walked around with his thumbs stuck in those tight pockets and looked at everyone as if he had a purebred horse right behind him, neighing expensively. Moreover, he didn't believe in God. Not because our textbooks said that God didn't exist, but because no one had proved to him that there was a higher power. And by the time Armstrong and Aldrin stepped out onto the moon, Gvidas was absolutely sick of the topic of God. I remember very well how grandmother, grating potatoes in the kitchen, would always pray and pray—that Grandfather wouldn't drink; that my mother's arm, which still hurt after its fracture, would heal; that our undependable father wouldn't leave us for good . . . And though God didn't fulfill a single one of her requests, and though even with my head pointed right at heaven I still couldn't smell the sweat from His feet, I continued to believe in Providence, not Gvidas. Once, losing his patience, he told me about the Ganges—which I'd already heard about from my older cousin. Religion convinced people to wade out into that holy river of India, hoping it would heal their wounds, and then they ended up dying from even worse infections. How can you argue with facts like that? I sat on the school bench with tears in my eyes and said nothing. Gvidas opened the classroom window, jumped out onto the field, picked two handfuls of dandelions, and then came back to present them to me like a prince showing kindness to his vanquished foes. The teacher put a remark about disruptive behavior in red ink on his report card, even though he'd wiped his footprints off the windowsill long before class started. We never argued about God again, and started celebrating our birthdays together. Shortly thereafter, Gvidas's mother's second husband, a very nice man—an officer, in fact—adopted Gvidas. On one birthday, Gvidas gave me a burnt-wood engraving he had made himself, showing a tiny cottage, a well, and a sparrow on a fence, probably chirping; and his stepfather took us out to see real military planes. Up until then I hadn't even known there was an airport in our little town. The planes there were little too, painted in a nonthreatening, potato-like color, but we were assured they could be deadly in the right circumstances. According to Gvidas's stepfather, all our enemies lived in America, probably in the same house as that Mr. Powers. On our way home, both of Gvidas's shoes filled up with snow (but not mine, because I was walking in his footsteps), and he soon came down with pneumonia. By the time he came back to class, I wasn't there to greet him, because I'd been transferred to a school closer to home, but for a long time I couldn't fall asleep nights because I would imagine Gvidas's suffering in his own bed—a sparrow chirping in each of his lungs. When he graduated from university, Gvidas got married, and then got divorced a few months later. Then he quickly married again, a Lithuanian born in America, and moved to Philadelphia. A classmate from my old school told me all of this. I saw Gvidas live only once, "twenty years after," as Dumas would say . . . On our lunch break from work at the journal, a girlfriend and I went out to a nearby restaurant. Gvidas was sitting there in a corner of the room. I don't doubt it was his wife sitting next to him: wearing earrings with diamonds and a short fur jacket that didn't at all suit a place where drunken artists with cold gray eyes slouched over three-cornered tables, propping themselves up with their elbows. The woman's face seemed cold, arrhythmic, out of sync with the world around it; I wished the gleam of her earrings could have been in her eyes instead . . . Gvidas dawdled over the menu and picked out dishes quite theatrically—one thumb stuck still stuck in his jeans pocket, the same as when he was a kid. I was still pregnant that day, enormous. Of course, it would have been interesting to hear first-hand what Grandfather hadn't managed to tell me about America. And if Gvidas's wife hadn't been sitting next to him, I would have gone over and started asking questions, about America, about all sorts of things. Whether dandelions grew where he lived; if he remembered how badly wool socks chafe the feet when both your shoes are full of snow; if he still burned pictures of sparrows on fences into wood . . . Clearly it wasn't the salad I was eating that was nauseating me, but rather this sudden flood of memories and feelings (I only have the one burnt-wood engraving, and I've kept it to this day). But I didn't go over to him. I needed to avoid stress, after all. Yes, I was working in a comparatively quiet office—all I needed to do was some light editing of our articles, and occasionally I had to select some suitable piece of prose to fill a gap—but, still, even in those days, everyone was expecting a catastrophe at any moment.

At night, past the windows of the dormitory where I lived with my husband, Soviet tanks rumbled into the city. The dormitory was a five-story building standing on a hill; the ground would shake so much from the passing of those tanks that our windowpanes would rattle as though it was hailing, and in the mornings we'd often find dirt on our windowsill blown up to us from several floors down. My husband, like so many other people, went to stand vigil by the Parliament night after night. I begged him not to. But every morning—he'd return. Setting an empty thermos on the table, he'd pile some tattered books not of this century into his briefcase and leave for work. As I learned later, women with small children, even a pregnant woman, were seen walking around inside the Parliament building during those days. They would put on their makeup every morning, and it seemed they weren't at all afraid of death. As for me, at night, I would turn on the radio. At first, before the radio station was occupied, I'd listen to the local news; later it was Radio Free Europe, and then those broadcasts that began, "The Voice of America is speaking" . . . Both here and abroad, Lithuanians were waiting for something—a very ordinary thing, in fact, that they might well have considered their due: namely, that the great countries of the world would, and as soon as possible, officially recognize Lithuania's independence . . . but instead the pleasant voices of all those men and women on the radio kept going on about the US president's important meetings with X or Y, and his concerns about Kuwait. True, he frequently said that the United States's relationship with the Soviet Union was important, not just to his country, but to the entire world. And then sometimes some other important person—not the president—would declare that those same relations could be damaged by recent events in the Baltic.

After the night of the massacre, a neighbor who'd seen it all from close up stopped in to see us. While telling us about it, he looked at my husband and me as if we were glass goblets from a set that had never been used. At night, when a song about freedom would occasionally interrupt the news, I would run to vomit in the shared toilet at the end of the dormitory hall. I tried very hard to retch quietly, so the neighbors wouldn't hear. I vomited every night, even though the child was already moving around inside me, and I ate only fruit, because everything, even bread, looked like meat to me now. Feeling sorry for myself, I was sorry for Gvidas too, sorry that he, coming from Philadelphia, had never suspected what sorts of inconvenience were awaiting him here. The trolleybuses ran infrequently; there were barricades made out of building materials standing in the streets. At night, factory sirens would go off without warning. Much later, I saw a documentary film about those days. They filmed everything, even what was going on in Parliament. The sequence where a priest blessed everyone who refused to leave seemed masterfully performed. And I was intrigued by the episode during which the leader of our country was waiting for a long-distance connection to America. When he spoke to the crowd through his window, he always stayed calm, but there in his office, when the call came through, he shouted into the receiver like everyone else. Not that I think I'd have done any better. How does one politely tell the president of the Freest, Most Just Nation—quickly, succinctly, and in a language not your own—that there are tanks running through your country crushing women, men, and children? On the other end of the line, it might have come through as a sufficiently proper request for aid, but in the office there reigned an absurdly industrious willingness to die.

It was around that time a friend at work loaned me a book of short fiction by a Lithuanian émigré—but she would only let me keep it for a couple of days. I managed to skim through only one story, but felt it suited the Easter issue of the journal perfectly. Since, in the January issue, we'd run interviews with the close friends and family of the victims of the massacre, in white letters on a black background (so that they were as difficult to read visually as they were emotionally, as it were), a change of pace seemed desirable. Even though the book of stories had been published in Chicago, and a very long time ago—long enough, according to Soviet copyright, that it was in the public domain—I decided to write to the author, who was still alive, to ask for her permission. A month later I got a package in the mail. It came from the very place where, when I was a child, it had seemed my grandfather was pointing at with his bent forefinger: Florida, a town not far from Miami. Along with the letter, the writer had added two photographs and a cassette of her own reading of a different story. One of the pictures was of her, the other of the town where she lived. The woman's dress was exactly the same color as the ocean in the other photograph. She was smiling— the way both ordinary women and the president's wife smile in that country. As I looked at those two pictures, it seemed completely clear to me that in resort towns like that there were people walking around who weren't at all like us—people with different biographies, differ- ent experiences. When they come here, you recognize them imme- diately because of their brightly colored clothing and the aspirated consonants in their speech. Without reading her letter, I put the cas- sette into my tape recorder. (The story was suitable for both children and adults.) The woman had written about "the old days," when she lived in Kaunas before the Second World War. At first glance (or hearing), the story seemed fragmentary, but all of the impressions were unified by a child's perspective: these were her everyday experi- ences. The girl in the story was then hardly bigger than the poppies growing next to her parents' house . . . Her dead grandfather lay in a coffin. His shirt was exceptionally white, and a rosary drew a dotted line between his frozen fingers. To the girl, her grandfather wasn't at all frightening. No, books of fairy tales were much worse . . . not that she read them, really; she much preferred looking at the colored pic- tures, even though, when no one was at home, it got scary: The witch with orange hair and the dragon with three heads on its disgusting neck seemed to come to life; they would sneak away from their pages in the book and stand behind the girl, staring.

The girl played in the courtyard next to the house, jumping from a cement ledge into the meadow with the other children. Once she fell on a rock hidden in the grass and scraped her leg. All the children, frightened at the blood, ran away, but the neighbor's boy picked her up from the ground. He wet a plantain leaf with spit, pasted it on the girl's knee, and told her to keep it in the sun for a bit. Then he picked two handfuls of dandelions, because the girl was standing in the grass barefoot with tears in her eyes and a runny nose. She didn't call the boy by name, but she remembered him like a prince—a moon shone on his forehead, and there were stars twinkling on each temple.

Later, a foreign army occupied Kaunas. Soldiers waded through the red poppies in the garden one morning, looking for something or other. The girl's mother pulled the curtains, closed the shutters, and told her daughter to speak in a whisper, but the soldiers broke inside nonetheless. With kicks of their boots they opened all the suitcases, packed for an escape abroad, and with their bayonets they stabbed through all the pillows . . . To the girl, at the end of the story, opening her eyes, the floating feathers looked like snowflakes. Instead of falling outside the window, they descended on her still-warm pillow and fell into the brown glass vase that had been left behind on the table.

In her letter—written on a computer and then printed out—the author told me that the story I had selected for the journal and the story she had recorded on the tape were from the same collection. The book had apparently won some American-Lithuanian literature prize, once upon a time. I'd like to get that book back so I can read the rest of it. It probably won't be easy to find. Even among the few readers left, people aren't much interested in local color now. Those who still read books only collect rare ones, brought from afar. Everyone wants to learn something new.

Essential Changes

I can't help but notice that the things which have gathered in my purse now are the same as the ones I remember in my mother's purse thirty years ago. Except that she carried her pills in a little pocket, while I carry mine in a special box for tablets. Now the handkerchiefs in my purse are paper; back then, mother had percale.

In the kitchen, the salt has begun hardening into a rock more often than before. I don't know why. Perhaps I used to wash it out more often than I do now. On the other hand, if you leave jam sitting around, it doesn't get moldy as fast as it did when I was a kid. Maybe because of the preservatives? And my daughter won't go to the movies with me anymore, but she's started daubing on my lipstick and wearing my boots. When she was younger, and she wasn't feeling well, I used to ask her if maybe she'd eaten a whole bag of potato chips again . . . but nowadays, a very different question flashes through my mind—is she pregnant?

Over the course of two years' worth of evening naps, the cat, lying on the mouse pad next to our computer, learned one simple thing: that it was fun to bat the mouse with his paw. At first, I suppose, he'd moved it accidentally, but later these interventions became premeditated and precise. Sometimes he would even set challenges for himself, for example trying to smack the mouse with his eyes closed—which is no mean feat. As was written in a story about a different cat, "He needed to bend his foot in a particular way, because otherwise all you would hear was a clank instead of a clink. The cat kept trying . . ." Which is how my supposedly anonymous comments about the play that won the National Prize this year wound up posted with my real name and personal e-mail address appended at the news site delphi.lt . . . Since my post was made up of Russian (and a few laconic American) swearwords, I was so ashamed I couldn't sleep for nearly a week. As punishment, the cat spent three days shut up in the cabinet under the sink. With a box of litter, a bowl of water, and a dish of cat food—but no remorse. In fact, he played the victim: he ate his litter, pooped on his food, and made histrionic choking sounds.

I've pretty much stopped watching television. Not that I ever watched very much. Every weekend all they would show were

American movies advertised as about "the will to win, the instinct to survive, and the power of love, no matter the cost." By then, this same country—the most powerful in the world—had already been waging a war on terrorism for several years, yet they were forever organizing roundtables in order to define that very phenomenon. And then, just before Christmas, my neighbor came over to see me, rising disheveled out of the dark stairwell bearing a lit candle, apologizing that she wouldn't be able to buy me a present this year, but offering the consolation that there was a man on TV who sounded very confident, interrupting the regularly scheduled programming no less, announcing that terrorism, the plague of the twenty-first century, would meet its final defeat this coming Monday night at the hands of Bruce Willis. That same evening I stuffed my television inside my grandmother's lilac embroidered pillowcase and set it in the kitchen. I sit on it when I'm peeling potatoes for my daughter. Or skinning fish for the cat.

Now I go to the movies more often. Usually on Fridays. I pick a late show, and go on foot. I like it when all that's left of your contact with the city is the wind on your face and the sound of the shoes of passersby. When all that's left of the choices the city offers you is solitude; all that's left of its light is the luminescence reflected off of the snow; and all that's left of its noise is the distant rumble of automobiles. Incidental phrases heard on the street arrange themselves effortlessly into coherent stories without endings. The theater smells like popcorn, perfume, and the plastic carpeting. Once upon a time, it smelled of sunflower seeds, wet umbrellas, and wine. Occasionally, you hear lines in the movies that some people feel accurately represent contemporary relationships, like: "Men love women as much as the women let them." Not long ago I read in a magazine that as many as twenty-eight percent of modern couples prefer to make love on the dining-room table; twelve percent at work, in the boss's office (when he's not there); three percent at work, in the boss's office (when he *is* there); thirty-five percent in the bathtub, amid floating candles; and sixty-four percent in the bedroom. Adding up all these percents, however, I got 142. Perhaps the magazine had taken into account the likely predilections of all the offspring that might be produced by these encounters? By the way, Italian researchers at Pavia University recently invented a tomographic test that can determine whether a person is really in love or just faking it—they arrived at this procedure when it was discovered that feelings of "legitimate" love increase the number of NGF molecules in a subject. Of course, this makes little difference, in the long run; even when love is "true," it only lasts about a year, they say, and when it comes time for couples to separate, their feelings don't even enter into the conversation—they leave it all up to their therapists. Speaking of marriage, I read that a woman in Israel married a dolphin. She wore a silk dress to the ceremony, and a pink diadem. When the dolphin swam up to the side of the pool, she kissed him, said, "I love you," and then dived into the water with her clothes on.

Despite the progress of modern science these days in analyzing inscrutable things like love, psychics are still able to make decent livings—searching for missing people (or their remains), predicting the future, and generally encouraging people to see day-to-day life as a many-tiered warren of sinister signs and symbols. For example, a psychic recently directed the police to a certain canal, and, sure enough, they pulled a girl's body—a suicide (or murder victim?)—out of the water: two years after she (the girl) had disappeared. The girl's purse looked like a black jellyfish, but was more recognizable than its owner. It's no less peculiar to me that writers too can manage to make a living from writing, these days, though their worldviews are considerably less intricate and interesting than those proposed by the psychics. That's why the reviews you see for so many books (for example, *There's a Curve—Don't Drive Off*) can just as well apply to so many others (for example, *A Woman Like That is a Treasure*).

Another sign of the changing times is that in the morning, people on the trolleybus chat on their cell phones with several passengers following along with their conversations involuntarily, including the driver: "Hello, Valera. No, I can't hear you either. I'm on my way now. I'm-on-my-way, *jomajo*, I said. Though after last night I don't really want to go anywhere. *Jele jele dusha v tele.* Unlock it. Carry the cement upstairs. Take everything upstairs, every last bit of that shit. Lock the place up. Don't let anyone out. I mean, don't let anyone drink. What . . . ? Unlock it. What . . . ? I've got the key?"

Sometimes our largest and most important newspaper runs

pictures of people who have donated their bone marrow to the sick. After the procedure, these donors have red bracelets tied on their arms. But, years ago, when goodness didn't call attention to itself, I knew a man and a woman, each of whom had donated a kidney to a loved one: The man gave his kidney to his wife, and the woman to her son. All four are still alive. The only things they wear on their arms are their watches. Speaking of kidneys, nowadays people are given to using the term "the kidney trade," referring to the practice of removing someone's organs by force. But to me, it brings to mind the red, white, and blue plastic boxes full of kidneys and livers at the Halė Market—same as it always has. When I go to work early in the morning, men in overalls are carrying those boxes out of vans, holding them in both hands, with a frozen carcass thrown over one shoulder . . . just as they did twenty years ago. Back then, there was always a diagram of a cow, divided into numbered sections, hanging in the larger meat stores, and their walls used to be covered in white tile. Always the same in every store. And at dawn, after it had rained, Bazilijonų Street—by the gates to the market—always ran with slightly pink water, traveling from the meat stalls to the gutters. Unless I simply imagined that. Or, more likely, I transposed it. Henry Miller wrote about a street where a veterinarian who castrated horses lived. And the bloody water I mentioned ran down that street, perhaps, in a city on another continent. I also see in the news that the threat of avian flu is considerably worse than anyone had anticipated. By the autumn, 250 swans had already died in the Volga Federal District, and before falling asleep I would imagine the locals wearing masks and rubber boots, plodding through a tulle of swans' wings, dragging the birds off by their necks, leaving wide trails in the tall dead bent grass.

On Sunday, the bells of Our Lady of the Gate of Dawn woke me the first time; the second time it was a reporter from that radio show, *The Second Program*. She asked me for a statement on gay men. I made my statement without getting out of bed. As I was talking, my daughter brought me some coffee. (At nine o'clock that morning, she'd put on my lipstick.) I didn't quite know what to say. That I enjoy their company? That they frequently have excellent taste? That they don't tend to humiliate or insult women the way "real" men do? I read recently that Elton John had married his long-time partner, and that the lapels of his tuxedo were rainbow colored. But you know, I went on, a friend's daughter (not gay) recently won tickets for herself and eight school friends to a well-known gay nightclub. Now, that might be a little much; a nightclub isn't an appropriate place for young girls. Why couldn't they win tickets to help with the restoration of the Ruler's Palace? Or a coupon entitling them to a free pizza? Or a gift certificate for the Vero Nova clothing store, which the young people seem to like so much? The reporter said, "Congratulations. For doing this interview, you've just won a ticket to that excellent film, *A History of Violence!*" And then she took a moment to reassure me about my friend's daughter. It turns out that on the first floor of that nightclub there's just a coffee bar and performance space. It's a hangout for a lot of young people, swingers, for example. Nothing sinister about it. My daughter immediately asked where the club was, then corrected me about that "cool" clothing store—it's actually called Terranova.

That so many of the changes occurring in the world have started to seem strange and inexplicable to me, that they've become a bit frightening, even shocking, I chalk up to one simple thing—that I'm growing hopelessly old. The mirror in the bathroom reflects this every morning. After coloring my hair, I don't even get two weeks of peace—the gray at my temples, banished who-knows-where, always return in force. And then, the bones in my feet have become a little deformed. In the evening I used to rub my legs down to the tarsi with a solution made according to an old folk recipe—razors dissolved in vinegar. There were still some straight-razor blades left over from Michailas. He was old fashioned all around, or at least as far as shaving and sex went. But he didn't shave every morning. For years I slept with wax balls—kneaded until warm—stuck between my toes, so my feet wouldn't warp too badly. To no avail. And before going to sleep I used to put Nyka-Niliūnas's two-volume diary on my stomach . . . but the muscles dwindled anyway. This is particularly noticeable when I bend over. My breasts look normal only when I hold them up from below. As soon as I pull away my hands, my chest would start looking as if it were on life support. Like one of Max Frisch's heroines, like hundreds, thousands of contemporary women,

I couldn't bring myself to look the way the mirror showed me. I'm really scared of surgeons, but yes, I've thought about it. The implants come in various sizes, shapes, and widths. If I remember correctly, from 100- to 800-cubic-centimeter implants increase the circumference of your breasts by 2.7 to 6 centimeters. (But wait a minute, is that right? Can volume turn into circumference? Breasts into a bra?) But, then, Botox for example—it's quick, it's easy; the toxin apparently gets absorbed in no time at all; you see results in ten days or less. You could get it all over with over your June vacation. Smooth out the wrinkles by your lip. Your nose. That big crease on your forehead—the one that makes you look twice your age. (You get one of those thanks to the death of someone close to you, or else staring at the sun too long without sunglasses.) And what about raising the corners of your lips? (When I was still a teenager, my aunt, the German language teacher, always told me, "You'd be a really pretty girl if you only smiled more often." With her sixth sense she'd already foreseen that in thirty years smiling would replace intellect in civilized countries.) And why not stretch your eyelids too, so, as they say in the ads, "the face acquires a naive look of wonder." Make all your skin smooth, matte. In fairy tales they say, "like alabaster." At the moment, the only times my skin is up to that standard is when there's a fog coming in, when I'm in the damp by a river, when I'm lit only by candlelight, or when I happen to be looking at an infant . . . Of course, you can bleach any old-age spots on your hands and face—no need for the scalpel. A colleague of mine once told me I'd gotten freckled in the sun over the summer—we were eating in a bright café with a glass roof. Only a person wholly oblivious to the passing years (or maybe I should say millennia . . .) could possibly mistake my spots for freckles. And the stretch marks on my stomach, I already know, are here to stay. When I gave birth, back in the twentieth century, three people hovered over me, talking over the events of the previous night, which seemed to interest them far more than me: the doctor, I mean, and the midwife, and the nurse—the latter holding a tin of instant coffee in her hand. During the night, you see, the border guards in Medininkai had been shot. On that hot July day, flies as heavy as military helicopters buzzed around the birthing center's used diaper pail. To me, it seemed both tactless and inappropriate for the doctor to be telling bloody stories full of the "will to win" and the "instinct to survive" when this certainly wasn't a Hollywood sort of scenario.

At around eleven o'clock at night, all the sounds in our courtyard die down. That's when the inanimate objects come to life. On the windowsill, the convolvulus plant's life gets more convoluted still; in the dark, I think it even dares to take a few steps out of its planter. Meanwhile, in the kitchen, a crushed plastic bottle regains its form with a snap. A shepherd in the bucolic landscape on a soup plate continues to drive his three lambs down a mountain path. They make a few millimeters' worth of progress . . . not that anyone will notice, come daytime. And then, the coats hanging by the front door, with their woolen mouths, discuss their impressions of the previous day in two different languages. My coat is Polish, my daughter's is Italian. Their voices have a human note to them, because the coats came from the Humana second-hand store. At this time of night I start feeling sad. Because of all the time I'd spent believing I could make time go backward. Embarrassed, I cover myself up to the eyes with a blanket and imagine writing a letter to my daughter from an expensive clinic, as I'd seen people do on reality shows about plastic surgery. "My darling daughter . . . if I don't make it through my operation, please know that I understood the risks, and that this is what I truly wanted. I'm tired of my real face. And, admit it, like all teenagers, you wish you had a younger-looking mother. And you're right. Lately, even the cat yawns as he watches me undress in the bathroom. Remember when you dressed me in your "Miss Sixty" sweatshirt to go to a New Year's party at Judita's, and what came of that? I didn't say anything to you then, but . . . if it weren't for that piece of clothing, perhaps the guest botanist would be my . . . our friend. He might have saved our mandarin tree, with its drying twigs, improvising a makeshift IV out of a bottle of mineral water . . . Remember the day of the military parade at Sereikiškių Park, when you had me try riding a skateboard, and I smashed a stranger's glasses with my wildly flapping elbow? (That was when we found out how much the glasses of an Independence Act signatory cost.)

"Of course, I'm only forty-six. It could be worse. And I still remember turning eighteen—well, a long, long time ago. I'm not sure I could even conceive of being forty-six, back then. We celebrated: Mama got oranges from somewhere, scooped them out and put apple mousse in the rinds. I sprinkled cinnamon on their whiteness—perhaps Nabokov would say like sand on snow—and with my finger sketched out my daydreams (in code) on the fogged-up kitchen windows. I thought, 'Eighteen already . . .' So, don't blame yourself for wanting me to be look younger; I want to be more attractive myself, or as they say now, 'sexier.' Unfortunately, they won't let you visit me here in the hospital. But believe me when I say I'll look unbelievable. Striking! And on television, too—for the first time in my life. Not that anyone will be able to recognize me. (I mean, in a good way.) Do me a favor—bring your skateboard over and leave it with the nurse (her name's Asta)—I'll ride home on it myself. The green traffic light at the intersection will go on shining for me, forever and ever. Amen. Your loving Mama."

These thoughts about the beauty that time has stolen from me haven't come to mind accidentally. Everyone should be able to control their thoughts. You see, before falling asleep, thinking about the numerous and horrible yet unavoidable things that happen to the elderly, in order to avoid needing sleeping pills, I intentionally concentrate on other changes, rather than these unpleasant ones. I mean those changes—not the minor irritations I've been going on about—that are really what I might call "essential."

. . . We bought the apartment where I've lived with my daughter for the past thirteen years from an old Polish lady called Malvina. The apartment's radiators had burst, but my husband and I only noticed this after we'd moved in, because, before selling her property, Malvina had carefully glued pieces of cast iron over all the holes. The apartment looked completely neglected, yes, but we liked the price and the location. After all, in the Old Town, everything's at hand. Sometimes the waitress in the café below would serve me a meat pie right through their open window, and I would hand my money to her the same way. And it was only a fifteen-minute walk to the university. My husband taught morphology there, in those days, and in his rather limited free time—just before dawn—wrote a dictionary of profanities. Unfortunately, I haven't been able to use a single word from that manuscript in this text. Not because the book was never published, and certainly not because of modesty, but because the terms he collected there are far too poetic and mild for the present day.

Malvina's son had worked at one of the first manufacturing cooperatives in independent Lithuania, which went bankrupt, and for several years afterward, washing the floor, I'd find signs of his defeat at the hands of the new economy in the cracks between the floorboards—plastic beads and buttons. And there were lines penciled in on one of the doorjambs. The child whose height those marks tracked probably has his own kids now.

One of my apartment's most interesting (or should I say extravagant) features is that it has two exits. One door opens into the inner courtyard. It was that door my husband left through when we separated. It was only after a couple of years that it occurred to me that quite a few of the people who left my apartment by that door, passing by the drying laundry in the yard, vanished without a trace. Sometimes I even suspected (though, obviously, I kept this theory to myself) that they had turned into blankets and coverlets hanging on the laundry line shared with the neighbors. A few weeks after a disappearance, strange notices, handwritten in ink, would show up in the passageway from the courtyard to the street: "We buy human hair—not less than ten centimeters long." Or: "We can remove your kidney stones without pain, using an amazing new method."

The other door in my kitchen leads via a shared hallway out to the opposite side of the building, toward the façade, past the broad stairway that takes us first to our mailboxes and then outside, into a busy street of gray smog. Not that we use the mailbox all that often, anymore; everyone uses e-mail, now.

On the opposite side of this hallway is another apartment. Exactly the same as ours. For most of our time here, Nobody lived there, creaking his calcified joints all night long, every night, starting promptly at eleven P.M. He only quieted down—temporarily defeated—when the owner let a student, a relative, spend the night in those two rooms that mirrored ours. In fact, I often thought it would be nice, if you could take off the roof, to see how we all slept, mirror images of one another, on different sides of the corridor, our feet nearly touching, like the figures on a pack of cards. Although, actually, the two figures on a single card are always the same sex, and their eyes are always open. The dilapidated hallway, soaked in old smells, whose four-meter-high walls present peeling nipples of wall-paper hanging like the petals of some tropical flower, is what divides the apartment into its two mirrored lives. During the Soviet years, the entire four-room space was a single courtroom. That's what our pharmacist neighbor told us, anyway. A Stalin painted in oils used to hang in our bedroom; later it was Lenin, and now it's Lenin again, right above my bed—just not the same portrait, of course. This one is three-dimensional, from a plaster mold. It dates back to an evening with friends that turned into a night and then a morning; while we were eating a healthy breakfast of four-grain porridge sprinkled with brandy, my friend the historian got out a drill and hung this bas-relief above my bed—he said he was doing justice to history. He hates change—as do I. Neither of us, for example, ever bought cell phones, and all our other friends, if they need to reach us in an emergency, just head out to wander the city, hoping to zero in on us by intuition.

The fact that our apartment had once been an important government institution would have been obvious to my husband and myself without the pharmacist. In the center of the door leading to the inside courtyard, at chest height, a small, thickly painted-over window is still clearly visible. During the Soviet years, people would hand in or receive important documents through that window. The employees on this side of the window, where my kitchen is now located—always smelling of the cat's fish and spices (coriander and ginger)—perhaps weren't even aware that from time to time their handling of those papers would take on the character of a judgment, steering their fellow citizens (without malice, and generally for no particular reason) toward heaven or hell. Stopping by that door, my cat would sometimes start hissing. Sniffing intently at the crack beneath the door and pulling his stomach in so far it seemed to be touching his spine, he would stand bristling in the shape of a question mark. (And now, come to think of it, perhaps my aforementioned—extremely infrequent!—disappearing houseguests also have something to do with that same door, that same little window.)

The last time my daughter went down to the mailboxes, she came back with an envelope. At first I thought it was the telephone bill, but then I saw that the envelope didn't have the transparent window through which the customer's name and address always peek. On the other side was handwritten "Good Friends Real Estate Agency" and the initials "B.N." I clumsily tore the letter while trying to open the envelope and had to fit the letter back together in order to read it. Some realtor, whose name had also been split in half, was writing to inform me that a buyer had finally turned up for the "mirror" apartment on the other side of the hallway. His telephone number was included. In order to buy the apartment, it seemed, he had to get my signature, because I had first refusal of those two rooms, given that the hall in between was considered a common area for the inhabitants of those four rooms. The sale couldn't progress without me. The realtor explained that she'd been trying to reach me at my home phone number, to no avail, and of course I had no cell number.

I immediately called the buyer, Vitalijus, who asked me to call him Vitia after we'd hardly exchanged two sentences, but I still wasn't quite certain what I wanted to do, and wanted to consider my options before heading over to a lawyer's with him. The signature was a formality, of course. The real decisions would come later. It would be necessary to divide up the common corridor, closing off the second entrance. Wall-over relationships. The plans of the building would need to be redrawn, since the common space would be redefined as private. And this would have to be confirmed at the registrar's office. Which would cost money. And then, obviously, I would lose my second entrance. This was definitely a problem, and in considering my future relationship with the neighbor, it might even be considered a deal-breaker. To get to the mailboxes we'd have to snake around through the inner courtyard and out into the smog of the dusty street. And I really did prefer to go via the stairs, in tights, in my nightgown, in the morning—not yet awake, without my teeth in yet, blinking in the dawn light of Aušros Gate Street coming in from outside. I hate making decisions. It's nearly impossible for me. And, if I remember correctly, it's always been that way.

When I was a child, we used to play this game with a ball: throwing it up in the air, you had to scream the name of a city, like a password, before it hit the ground. The other children always had to pick my city for me, because I would freeze on the lawn, the ball pressed to my beating heart, while in my memory the name of my hometown would flash in tiny lights. (No doubt psychologists have some name for my condition.) It seemed to me that by choosing any city other than my hometown, I would be—in some way I can't explain—betraying certain things from my past. For example, the hides my grandfather cured after the war . . . the eternally pregnant Rudokienė (as a child I thought that all the people in town came from her belly) in her heavy black wool coat . . . not to mention her white scarf, woven on a square board, almost as big as a table, rimmed with nails. Leaving my grandparent's house in the winter, laughing, she would slide down from the hill toward the river on her rear end. Like Aidas Marčėnas wrote, "The river was simply like a vein through which my childhood flowed." And then there was my godmother. Her father died in Canada and left her an old set of wine goblets with hunting scenes. They were made with cut glass, so that they would be easier for the men in the autumn forest to handle with leather gloves. Maybe even while sitting on horses. The set probably came from some large European city, brought all the way to Canada. And then, after a hundred years or so, it returned. To a small town.

Once again unable to choose, as though the ball was in the air above me, about to come down, I got a bit hysterical, perhaps from over-thinking the situation. I decided that even if it wasn't ethical, it would be best for me to end the story of the apartment division before it even began. Vitia would, without a doubt, come over to look over the inside yard from my apartment . . . maybe even with a bottle of champagne. Although he'll praise the sandwiches I'll make him, he won't take this pretense too far; he won't figure on seeing much of me after he moves in. Only one thing will really matter to him: is there room in the yard to park an old BMW? On weekdays, anyway. Because he had already told me during our first conversation that he didn't have a rented space in the city. And the first thing I'll notice about him will be his almost entirely shaved head and the scar on his left ear. (I'll immediately think of a character in *A History of Violence*, which I've just seen.) Other than these features, however, Vitia will have a gentle look about him, a "Lenten face." I'll suggest he go ahead and have a look at the courtyard. Swallowing the words "what do you think?" I'll say, instead, "have a look, Vitia." And wave my arm at the window. (And if fear of this plan being implemented doesn't paralyze me, I'll attempt to make this movement appear careless, womanly, graceful.) The Halė Market is very nearby, I'll tell him—meat, livers, kidneys . . . and a store with empty shelves. I'll look at his shaved head and add that across the street is a barber who works with dull tools. And some bums. A prostitute or two. They ply their trade in cars and near the Aušros Gate, too. Closer by, in the inner courtyard, there's smog, of course; it's not just the pansies that wilt, it's the dogs too. During holidays the courtyard is frequently spattered with vomit. There's a hostel for foreigners right here, you know. We get all sorts of pilgrims . . . Japanese, Polish, Muslim . . . actually, we're quite a high-risk zone for terrorism, given that we're so close to the Gate. With all the tourists, sometimes there's fourteen cars parked in the courtyard on summer evenings. And Vitia will get up from the table and head over to the window, saying, "Cool it. I was born nearby, on Tyzenhauzai Street. But, even so, there's no way so many cars could fit in there . . . you're laying it on pretty thick." And then it would be very handy if Vitia made a mistake. Albeit one I will have "choreographed" for him in advance. A bit nervous, despite his bluster, he'll show his pedantic streak, wanting to go out and count the cars in the courtyard, just to show me up. Right away, in fact. He'll stand up, swallow a last bite of sandwich the way a python swallows a rabbit, and walk out into the courtyard . . . into the courtyard he'll walk . . . through *that* door. "One, two, three, four, five, seven," I'll hear him say from below, "it's only early evening and there are ten cars here already . . . damn." After which Vitia will approach the drying laundry. He'll walk right up to the blankets and coverlets . . . standing between him and the setting sun, they'll look red instead of white or varicolored . . . they'll flutter in the wind like the flames of hell . . . and soon, all that will be left of Vitia is a voice counting off the last few cars. Then, after looking down the stairs, I'll close the door (with its painted-over and nailed-shut window at the height of my chest) without making a sound. The cat will greet me, a bristling question mark. Smiling forgivingly, I'll offer him some boiled fish that I'll have prepared ahead of time. I'll ask my daughter if she's done her homework. In turn she'll ask me if the man buying the apartment seemed okay. For a week or two it'll be quiet, or at least as much as it is in the evenings after eleven o'clock at night. Once again, Nobody will start creaking his rusty joints beyond the wall. Then the agent B.N. will call and ask if I happen to know where my future neighbor has gone. "He didn't seem like the drinking type," she'll say. "A drunk wouldn't have gotten a loan like that, or work where he works . . ." "Where does he work?" I'll ask calmly, but B.N. will hang up. A week later, an announcement, written by hand, in ink, will appear in the passageway: "For one low price, we will make a monument out of Karelian granite to commemorate your loved ones—or yourself! Choose from a range of elegant astrological symbols!"

When I wasn't feeling quite so morbid, I'd think along these lines: a single square meter of a similarly neglected apartment in a similar Old Town neighborhood would go for about three thousand litai. Perhaps I'll make Vitia a deal on my half of the common space. He would be absolutely delighted, I'm sure. And then, all that would remain would be to brick over the door from my kitchen to the common corridor. This might even result in an interesting effect. I could go over to the door, open it, and be faced with a dead-end plastered wall. I should think up some truism, some especially compelling thought to paint on that wall. I'll get about twenty-five thousand litai, I'll convert them to euros, and have teeth put in that I don't need to take out at night . . . At the very least, I'll have convinced myself that volume has the power to turn into circumference. But let's say I didn't succumb to the temptation to sell that space after all. Perhaps I could make a storage space out of the eight square meters of my half of the corridor—to store books in, and shoes, and my long-dead grandmother's Singer sewing machine. She bought it at the beginning of the twentieth century and used to travel through many Lithuanian villages with it, sewing. Many people associate Singer sewing machines with their loved ones. The most intimate story I've heard about a sewing machine was told to me by a carpenter, now dead. He was making bookshelves for my husband at the time. He told me the story over the telephone, drinking a second bottle of Georgian wine he'd uncorked by smacking the bottom with his fist; I heard the blow over the receiver. He was sitting at home, alone. He couldn't go get the corkscrew because his leg was hurting really badly that day. Earlier, he had said that when they finally amputated, it would take him only a few days to make himself a wooden leg, hollow on the inside. Out of a pine growing by his mother's grave. But then, as he drank, he thought up another excuse for having opened his bottle in that macho way; he said he'd wanted to check if his hands were as strong as they were in his youth. And then came his story. Which was terrifying, frankly. Because all stories in which the main characters are time, a person's loved ones, and objects that come to life are horrible. But, you know, it was very well told. A piece of perfect storytelling. And just as I was opening my mouth to ask him to let me use a detail of his story in my own work—before I had even begun a coherent sentence, merely pronounced the little word "maybe"— the carpenter interrupted me in his calmly masculine way and said, "And don't you dare ever even try to tell that story to anyone else." I was ashamed.

Lately, getting old so much more quickly than is proper, I hear the clatter of my grandmother's sewing machine more and more often. Then other things "glue" themselves to the sound: a ficus, the smell of potato pancakes, and she herself. She keeps tucking a strand of her hair behind her ear. As if she were voting before an unseen audience at a Soviet Congress, from time to time she slows the sewing machine by holding back the hand wheel with a raised palm. She curses out her crooked stitches in Russian. Nowadays, the Singer lives in a friend's house—a remote single-family house in Pavilnys. Inside the Singer's base, in a veneered space, were kept two thimbles—one of brass and one of iron. Grandmother called them *noparskai*. On her name day, February 16th, St. Ona's, the thimbles, quietly clinking in the dark, would drink, one from the other, the last drops of the sewing machine's oil, then curl up to drowse in a narrow torn-off little piece of hide once cured by my grandfather. It's funny, but I think I'd like to be buried there, I mean back home, denying the modern world (or perhaps simply scorning it), and as close as possible to my loved ones and the things of my childhood, even though this isn't possible. I've been living in the capital for forty years now. When I die they'll take me to Rokantiškės cemetery.

When I think I've scrupulously weighed every single possibility, as far as the division of the corridor, I meet with Vitia. I'd only ever seen him from a distance—at the lawyer's, sitting with the old owner of the apartment. He didn't come over to my place—he went straight to his half of the apartment. With a friend. Whom he introduced as Petrarka. Undoubtedly his name was actually Petras. And this Petrarka smiled, setting a bottle of schnapps and two plastic glasses (the words we use for such vessels have never made any sense to me) on a stool in Vitia's empty living room, not saying a word. He was the sort of person who only speaks when something surprises him. And gets surprised only rarely. Petrarka scratched at the wallpaper, but when he found another layer of paper under it, and then another, and after that, quite unexpectedly, yet another, he poured himself some vodka. Vitia really had been born on Tyzenhauzai Street, but didn't otherwise correspond to my imaginings in any respect—short, stocky, a bit plump, like a former athlete; with a sad, sly smile, not at all a "Lenten face." His goatee, fastidiously shaved every morning, was an exceptionally poor match with his rough palms. Which is when I realized that he'd spent approximately fifteen years leading another sort of life entirely. Perhaps one that wasn't quite legal. And because his past didn't correspond to his present, yet another option for dividing the apartment shot into my head. In essence, I had only one question left for Vitia, so I asked it: "Have you bought this apartment as an investment, or to live in?" He answered, "I've gotten divorced from my wife, and I'm buying this apartment to die in. I'm just a bit short on space and money." That's what I thought. Space and money are in short supply for almost everyone, even someone prepared to die. So I asked him to come over to my side of the building and, very efficiently, without witnesses, without emotion, I laid out the third possibility for dividing the apartment. Which is to say, I offered eight square meters of space to a man whose past didn't correspond to his present. In the Old Town. Without asking for a dime. (But in exchange for a single service.)

When we quietly returned to Petrarka a half-hour later, he was sitting on the windowsill, completely drunk, cleaning out his fingernails with a foot file—I have no idea where he got it. Vitia called him a taxi. Petrarka went down the stairs, continuing his cleaning. I wouldn't have been surprised if he would have finished his manicure by sticking the file into the taxi driver's heart. He seemed horrifyingly inert.

Vitia and I gradually finished the vodka, but now we'd set up camp on my side of the hall. Vitia, like all real or imaginary men, really did inhale the sandwiches I made . . . but real men usually only eat that way after a day of exhausting work, out of hunger. Well, Vitia was eating after difficult work too—just not work with his hands. Work that was difficult because it was nerve-wracking. At nine o'clock in the evening I saw him out to Aušros Gate Street. *Not through the courtyard door . . .*

Returning, I stopped at the café for some kharcho soup, because one thing that always sobers me up fast is getting a little tomato paste flowing in my veins in place of blood, and so I began then to go over every recent choice, legal or otherwise, in my head. Nearby, several men were eating meat pies. A random scattering, sitting singly or two together at a table. Like wax figures with orange vests. Judging from their clothes, they were the workers putting in a new road next to our building, along the railroad. In preparing their location, they had to excavate a section of the hill running parallel to the tracks, where I used take the cat in summertime, kick up clouds of dust on the footpaths, read, and sunbathe naked. The first thing they found when they started digging was that there were a lot of people buried there, about a meter down. One of my neighbors from the next street over even sent me, via computer, a picture he'd taken—half-excavated skeletons tangled up with tree roots, as if they were lovers. On my left, in the café, next to the window looking out onto the busy street, sat one man, alone, who didn't in the least resemble the workers. He looked conceited. He reminded me somehow of Victor Pelevin. Black glasses and boots laced up to the knees. He couldn't be in Lithuania, though—the author, I mean; I don't watch television anymore, but I'm sure I would have read about a visit like that in at least three newspapers. Aside from that, however, it wasn't too difficult to believe that he'd come snooping around a dive like this in search of homemade soup and homespun characters . . . When the waitress approached this man, he took off his glasses and said, in Russian, "When I was a child, I used to eat a Lithuanian dish called *vėdarai*. Do you have it?" I immediately remembered a short sentence from one of Pelevin's stories in *A Werewolf Problem in Central Russia*: "Happiness in general is nothing but reminiscence." This story describes the ontology of childhood: a child's impressions of growing up in a prison. The walls, a game he plays in the corridor, and the light falling through a high window are the only events of the story. I finished my soup, went home, and then I called my friend in Pavilnys.

I have reasons for not wanting to mention my friend's name, first or last. (Last even less than first.) It will suffice to say that after Mother died, I took her Singer over to my friend's house along with a pile of half-necessary, mostly Soviet books that wouldn't fit in my apartment. Our friendship was cemented by three years of working at the same journal, and is, nowadays, a relationship of absolute trust. Yet, our goals, our opinions of men, stockings, hobbies, perfumes—none of it matches. She used to say: of all the wines in the world, brandy is the best, and she used to call that Russian company out to gobble up Lithuania's one oil refinery "Fuckoil." She was a fan of Coco Chanel, but she would intentionally mispronounce it as "Sinel," the word for the rough homespun coats worn in Siberia. Instead of saying "make love" she'd say "lie down next to." My husband couldn't stand to be around her because he hates rude women who smoke, not to mention corny jokes. I, on the contrary, have an affinity for corny women and rude jokes. I would frequently walk through the Old Town with her in the rain. Unless there had been some catastrophe, or one of us needed some important advice from the other, we never really called. Although, actually, sometimes she'd call me for no reason at all, but then only very late at night. I would pick up, and, after taking a smoker's pause, my friend would ask without preamble if I knew what *paella* was, or what the English word was for a business where you could hock an antique white-gold ring with an emerald setting—who knows what it was all about, maybe she did crossword puzzles when she couldn't sleep. I liked the way she always mixed up her prepositions, telling me how one of her rich Pavilnys neighbors "dressed out and went up." Sometimes, when I called her, she would hang up on me almost immediately, first explaining that she didn't see any sense in life today, and I knew it was useless to pry—it would just make her mad. Once, when we'd only recently met, I invited her to go to the movies. She refused: "I haven't been to the movies in twenty years and I won't break the tradition. The last good movie I didn't see was Fellini's *And the Ship Sails On.*"

At the time, I wrote for the journal we both worked at, while my friend was an accountant. They threw her out, supposedly because they'd discovered she never finished her college degree, but actually because of her endless sick days. First they cut off one of her breasts, then the other. Now she doesn't do anything, she just waits. For a spot to appear on her lungs. And it was around the time her husband left her for a colleague who could provide solace from all his family's misfortunes. Perhaps there's no need to condemn him—when their wives become ill, husbands take forever to recover. I won't call his lover names, either—she sincerely wanted to help. People say excessive empathy is a mark of exceptional delicacy. When I visited my friend in the hospital, she would scribble letters on toilet paper, put them in envelopes, seal them, and give them to me to drop in a mailbox. They bore the name and address of a man I didn't know, as well as the words "Open when necessary." When they discharged her from the hospital, we waited for a taxi together in Santariškės for about an hour. My friend sat on a bench and looked at a bush blooming with exceptionally bright, yellow spring flowers. At that time of year, those bushes are usually the only impudently bright plant on the otherwise completely green background of spring. She asked me: "How do you measure your life?" I answered, in my daughter's age and height. "I measure mine in seconds," she said. I said, don't be upset, people go on living without their legs, arms, or memories. And a good number walk around without hearts, and never even know it. My friend smiled: "It doesn't make me feel better just because I know that someone else has it worse." After thinking it over, I realized why she never went to the movies. You couldn't sit through them if you really counted your way through life second by second, as my friend claimed she did. No, you'd stare up at the screen, dividing hours into minutes, minutes into seconds, seconds into half- or quarter-seconds, never getting caught up with the plot or the characters' problems. It would be a joyless endeavor.

Shortly afterward, they fired me as well. It's funny . . . If I had to say why, I'd say: because I couldn't live without *Stilius*, the fashion magazine. I've read it from volume one, issue one. It makes everything look so sexy and new, and everything—children, glasses of champagne, puppies, flowers, toothbrushes in people's hands—look so happy. It particularly pleases me that many of the people featured in its pages are involved with charities—spreading kindness (and money) throughout the world. They arrange meetings with one another at the opera and dine leisurely on stone terraces overgrown with climbing plants; before sleeping together, they massage each other with oil, and then make love as lightly and softly as organza. As long as I was turning the pages of that magazine, I really did believe that time could stop. That I could greet spring, carefree and beautiful. That I could greet it, period. In one of its earliest issues, I found the following advice (other magazines of that era—all of them behind the times—wouldn't even mention the horror of cellulite): "If you notice that the skin in the area around your thighs and seat is sagging, don't be frightened. Do an experiment—it costs nothing. With the dull end of a pencil, poke yourself in the bottom; if an dimple remains, you should be concerned." Next to this article was a photo of a dimpled orange peel, the name of a cream, and a picture of a woman who resembled Andie MacDowell. As I was looking at all of that, my editor, with one knee on her desk, was opening up a window. We were sitting with our graphic designer in an Old Town attic space, in front of a fan that wasn't doing a thing to make the heat more bearable. Completely spontaneously, and clearly without giving it any thought, I reached out and poked the dull end of a pencil in my editor's behind, and, before she came to her senses, lifted up her silk skirt—to find that there was a depressed dimple clearly visible on her sweaty bottom. But they couldn't fire me just for that . . . they had to think up something better. Thus, according to them, I left intact—and with malice aforethought—a rather unfortunate typo in an interview with the wife of a well-known politician ("ruling party" having become "ruling farty").

After the sixth ring, my friend picked up the phone in her kitchen.

"Today I'm not feeling very well. But fine, let's talk."

I heard her running water from the tap, dropping a metal implement, pouring something that gurgled as it went. Clearly she was holding the telephone pressed to her ear with her shoulder.

"Can I ask you something?" I began. "I know you've already been thinking it over, so please don't take this the wrong way . . . but, where do you want to be buried?"

Her voice immediately took on an economist's coldness: "Listen to me. Don't let yourself confuse the remodeling of your apartment with a disaster. Don't look at old photographs before you go to sleep. Or new movies. Don't lounge around in bed with your cat the way you would with a person. Better go and drink some brandy. On top of whatever you're already drinking."

I immediately took this the wrong way: "When I get upset, I drink white wine or nothing."

My friend said, "Sure, and the day I catch you drinking 'or nothing,' I'll make sure to get it on camera. Look: I've got a will. I wrote it after my operation, while I was waiting for the next spot to appear, on my lungs or liver. I want to be cremated."

"In Riga? Do you know how much that costs? Besides, don't think that'll get you out of anything—they'll still put you through all the paces first: embalming, a coffin, a wake, your face twisted into an expression you'd never have made while alive . . ."

"So, no funeral. Wrap me in foil and throw me in the oven.."

I know that many people might consider her an insufferable cynic, but—she isn't. She uses Russian puns and artificial crudity to save herself from her own exceptional sensitivity. She apparently thought I needed to suffer a bit, just now. I'll wait a bit, I thought, and maybe she'd start talking normally soon. What I needed most at this stage of my life was gentleness. And protection. In fact, I was familiar with my state of mind from a few years earlier—what I felt like was a cracked egg. I tried to change the subject:

"Yesterday, a neighbor came by and told me he'd celebrated New Year's in the country with his wife and grandchild. He's got a wooden cottage near Ignalina, I've told you about it. He fired up his stove, he said, chased away the cottage's eternal chill, cooked chicken and fish, drank some wine, then tried to call one son, and tried to call another, but the line was dead. Then he went to bed and rats started running around the place. He said, 'I looked up, and there, in the moonlight, like in a horror movie, there was one hanging from the child's bed . . .'

They were everywhere, he said—on the toys, on the books, the curtains, and on the food. At first he and his wife managed to scare them all off, but by the time dawn came around the squeaking had driven them so crazy that my neighbor got out his late father's shotgun . . . Can you believe it?"

"So . . . he shot one. What would you have done?" From her intonation I felt she was going to hang up on me any minute, but I couldn't stop:

"I wouldn't have done anything. The rats would have eaten me alive . . . and, speaking of which, I really need to tell you what you'll need to do when I die."

"If you only knew," she sighed, "how sick I am of this subject. Why has this become so important to you, lately, when you don't have any real reason to . . . ?"

"I read, recently, that a person sits on their death like they're sitting on a barrel of gunpowder, but goes ahead lighting matches anyway, flinging sins about like they're cigarette butts."

"So call your writer friends and let *them* listen to you go senile. What's death to a writer, anyway? A blow. What's a woman to them? A hole. When writers die, I'll tell you what should be done to them . . . why even bother dressing them up for the open casket? No, just glue their mouths shut, that's all the dignity they need. Listen: why don't you write down for me what you want me to do after you die. Okay? Whatever you want, I'll do. I'll even sign a contract. For a small fee . . ." And with that, she finally hung up. Until our next call (or, rather, hers).

That's easy to say, "write it down." But what could I possibly add to what I've already written? It seems I've already gone over it all. About growing old and withering away. Laziness, panic, and desperation. The forehead wrinkle you get from worrying too much over the deaths of loved ones, or from looking into the sun for too long without sunglasses. Old-age spots on the arms that the uninformed still manage to confuse for freckles. I've written about the inevitable solitude, that circle drawn around me by some unseen hand, that border only three creatures can cross without frightening me—the cat, my daughter, and Nobody. (Or, in order: my daughter, the cat, then Nobody.) About the impossibility of turning back time, and my total inability to adjust to essential changes—for example, the division of the common hall outside my apartment. All I could still do would be to produce an epilogue for my friend. In the nineteenth century, people were still relying pretty heavily on epilogues. Oftentimes you can't even figure out from the epilogue what had happened earlier— the writer, acting like a historian, reports on what had finally transpired, and to whom, in concise sentences full of information and drained of sentiment.

Not long ago, I read in the newspaper that 250 swans had died in the Volga Federal District over the autumn. And before falling asleep I would imagine the local inhabitants, with masks and rubber boots, plodding through a tulle of swans' wings, dragging them by their necks, leaving wide trails in the tall dead bent grass. Avian flu is considerably worse than anyone realizes. We might all die of it. But I feel like I've already mentioned that to someone recently. Maybe even today. Who was it? That's the first sign that I'm losing my memory. They say hardening of the arteries can lead to dementia. Cholesterol coats the veins like frost on power lines. I knew a relatively young woman who laughed when she was diagnosed. She died four months later. She spent her last three days awake, constantly demanding, shouting, day and night, that all the people in her refrigerator be taken out at once. She wrapped a head of cabbage up like a sick child and kept it on her pillow. No medication could put her to sleep.

EPILOGUE
Vitia's telephone number is +370 675 127 13. His apartment (on Olandų Street, or else Viršuliškės, next to the Church of Blessed Jurgis Matulaitis) has two exits. Just the same as in my apartment, but in my apartment the door from the kitchen to the hallway will already be bricked over; or, more accurately, it will still open inward, as it always has, but there will be a plastered wall behind it. Vitia started remodeling the following week. And, remember, I gave him my eight square meters of corridor. (For this epilogue.) The moment will come, in time, as funeral-home staff like to say, when "close friends and loved ones will be left alone in the viewing area to bid farewell to the deceased"—meaning, in this case, Vitia, you, and three of Vitia's men, standing around my coffin. Dressed, naturally, in black. And

with pasts that won't necessarily correspond to their present. One of these men will be Petras. Petrarka. He'll probably be the one who hangs around right inside the exit after all the staff file out. I know for a fact that my daughter won't want to be there at that moment; she was always afraid of dead bodies, even as far back as her grandmother's funeral. And yes, other people will undoubtedly attend the ceremony, but—perhaps it's wicked of me—they don't concern me in the least. Now: in "viewing areas" like this, there are almost always a few vases, a little table, a couple of chairs, multitudes of wreaths and flowers, and . . . another coffin. Yes, leaning against the wall; maybe even more than one; there are usually at least a few like that, just standing around, so it's easy enough to plant one ahead of time. Of course, if there's been a flu epidemic, there will be a lot more of them there, both open and closed. They say that if we're really hit hard, the undertaking business will thrive, at least at first, becoming the fundamental point of commerce in Western society; but then, soon enough, everyone will start getting buried in permeable polythene bags. Anyway, the two coffins—mine and the one leaning against the wall—will be switched by Vitia's three friends. The one I'm lying in will be shut without any farewells, and they'll lean it up against the wall, just like the other one. Whereas the other one will now be on the coffin stand. When the funeral home staff opens the door, you, my dear, cynical friend, will be standing weeping next to the closed coffin. Vitia will hold you by the elbow. I know that this moment will be the trickiest for you. It seems critical to me too. A week ago, I went out to look over my old home town Viršuliškės—I don't think it'll be as complicated as we imagine; I waited around for hours, saying my last farewells to two people I didn't know. Not long ago I read in the *Lietuvos Rytas* newspaper that one old lady found out after the funeral that the coffin she'd seen buried didn't actually contain her husband—despite the tiny size of the town, they were burying two people that day, and, well, these things happen.

To Vitia—you can depend on him—our little caper will seem somewhat archaic. Once upon a time, he made deals with the living, not the dead—and for far more money than the twenty-five thousand litai he saved himself by agreeing to participate in this plan. Which is exactly why his past doesn't correspond to his present. But his profession is archaic, too. Nowadays deals are done with the dead all the time—we're just spared the gruesome bits. Virtual or half-virtual wars are going on all over the world. Airplanes fly without pilots, or else, if you happen to get one that still has human beings aboard, they litter the ground with their bombs, they drop them on top of factories that supposedly contain centrifuges for concentrating uranium, and on cities and villages too, all the while looking at an electronic schematic glowing in the dark of their cabins. You can make a killing off of killing a thousand people without ever seeing a single tear or drop of blood. Without even looking behind you to see how prettily your explosives slide through the air to the ground below.

You will accompany my pseudo coffin to Rokantiškės together with everyone else: my daughter, Rūta, Margarita, her Juozas, some of my other friends . . . I don't, as you know, have any close family left, daughter aside . . . And when "my" coffin, not weighing more than it should (inside will be the two bundles of books I stored in your basement, along with my grandmother's Singer), descends into the pit, I know you'll cheer up. Because you'll be watching it all in the same way you watched the last good movie you didn't see twenty years ago. "And the ship sails on . . ." you'll think. You'll even get the urge to have some brandy. And then, one of my most "feminine" friends, the kind of woman you particularly dislike—Rūta perhaps, who's already managed to daub her so-carefully-conserved Eden perfume behind my ears during the viewing—will say, "Excuse me, I've been wanting to ask . . . Who on earth put her in that awful dress? So short, and so very tasteless! She never wore anything like that before." And through your clenched teeth you'll say, "It's Coco Sinel."

At that very moment, Petrarka will already be in a van, driving me—and not even speeding—back to my hometown. To a pit still being dug. Vitia and two young men will remain inside the van until the grave is ready. One of the young men will doze off. The other will be constantly tapping out text messages, but not about what's going on. (Not that he actually knows too much about what's going on.) The irregularly dug pit, intentionally without straight edges—as if intended for nothing more than burying a stinking heap of trash—won't be finished until evening. It's being dug by locals, but the coffin will be buried by Petrarka's group. In the woods by the river. Just about three kilometers from the spot where my grandfather's house once stood. And where, now, a few wooden cottages built by Vilnius Bank skulk in its place. Before easing in my coffin, Vitia will ask to have a peek. He needs to be in control at all times. He'll shine in a flashlight. But it's not necessary. I really will be in the coffin. Just the same as when they put me there. My face will be fair and smooth, and there won't be any wrinkles on my forehead. In fairy tales they would say, "skin like alabaster." That's the way skin should be in the fog by the river.

That evening, all three, excluding Vitalijus, will get drunk. For the time being, using their own money. Sometime around seven o'clock the following morning, Vitia will be the first at the hotel to wake up, kick away the scattered shoes and socks, boil water for tea in the dusty pot on the table, and then drive to the site of last evening's festivities to take, as Russian professional assassins say, a "control shot," to make sure the objective has been achieved. The ground will be cleared of yesterday's pine needles and trash. Taking his time, watching the swift river, he will smoke a cigarette. It will be almost quiet. Anyway, Vitia won't hear anything. Maybe just a train passing, very far away. A jay, a woodpecker. Tuk, tuk . . . But me—I'll hear something else entirely.

. . . Underground, my godmother's wine glass set with those hunting scenes will tinkle very faintly. I'll see the bird cherry blossoms falling on Vitia's thin leather jacket, clinging together, blown then into a white mass on the riverbank, resembling a scarf woven on a board rimmed with nails. For an instant, I'll even imagine that Vitia came into the world, into my mirror apartment, out of Rudokienė's belly. And then, deep in the ground, perhaps perched on the root of a tree, the carpenter who told me never to repeat his story will be working on his prosthetic leg. (Tuk, tuk . . .) He'll have propped the other leg, the remaining one, against who knows what. Maybe he'll stick it into some ground water. And Vitia will glance at the river again. Me too. But, as ever . . . we'll see completely different things. He'll notice the brown seaweed, still not recovered from the winter, waving in the current. But me—I'll see the sheepskins my grandfather tanned after the war bobbing there in the water, spreading out to the sides. The river, to me, is like a vein through which my childhood flowed. After stubbing out his cigarette on his heel, Vitia will check the soil density by kicking at it with his shoe. Then he'll get into the van and drive straight to an ATM. "In a jacket sprinkled with bird cherry blossoms, and smelling of a corpse," he'll approach the machine and take out two hundred litai for gas and miscellaneous. And will have no idea that—through the slot of the cash machine, supposedly from Vilnius Bank, but in reality straight from an old, demolished cottage—the money is being handed to him by my sleepy grandfather, wakened too early.

On the trip back, like on the way there, all four will ride in silence. Near Ukmergė, Vitia will take pity on Petrarka. Because he'll remember past hangovers of his own. Instead of driving straight down the freeway to Vilnius, he'll turn off by Ukmergė. In the café they'll drink Švyturys stout, likewise silently. In the silence, somewhere not far away, two shots will ring out. And this will be enough to surprise Petrarka, for once, and so he'll finally open his mouth: "It used to be that these stupid hicks would sit around shooting crows because they had nothing better to do, but now they've gone nuts because of the bird flu . . ." And it won't occur to any of them that it might have been shotgun fire, and that it might have been intended for a rat. Probably by some man whose instinct to defend, to guard his children and his woman, as well as his innate marksmanship, had been handed down through the centuries. After climbing back into the van, Petrarka will take the wheel and start to speed . . . Well, what of it? He's been driving with Vitia from the day he got his driver's license, but he's never gotten a ticket when they were stopped yet. He speeds just to speed, not because he's eager to get anywhere. Everyone will have been told a long time ago that they'll be paid back in Vilnius. But it's precisely now, during the drive, that Petrarka will find the time to be bored to death by the previous day's work. His thoughts will scatter; it will become impossible for him to concentrate. Besides, the scraped knuckles on his right hand will hurt . . . What had been the connection between Vitia and that lady next door? he'll wonder. It's all pretty unclear. Probably just money, or the craziness of some distant kinship, given the way families stick together in clans in Lithuania, because she was old and not pretty.

Petrarka himself wouldn't have gotten involved in all this, certainly not for so little money, if it hadn't been for that eternal debt of his. Which you couldn't even call a debt. He had reminded Vitia of it a thousand times when they were drinking. Once, Vitia had even suggested that he shut the hell up. Fifteen years ago, you see, next to the Tyzenhauzų Palace, four men had knocked Petrarka to the ground. They kicked him till they had broken two ribs and a collarbone, and his liver started pouring out the corner of his mouth. Anyway, that's how it felt. When he woke up in the hospital, that's just what he told the doctor: "My liver is leaking out." The nurse on duty started laughing, because they had indeed needed to put a bandage over the ripped skin at the corner of his mouth. But the thing was, if Vitia hadn't shown up at the gate at the right moment . . . well, no one would have. Sure, Petrarka's scattered, hungover thoughts, jumping around like a cloud of midges in the sun, could—if you really wanted to—be brought together into a coherent form. (Every line of thought must be controlled.) In essence, though without knowing it, Petrarka is thinking precisely the same thing that Victor Pelevin once wrote. Even though he hasn't so much as seen a single copy of the famous writer's books, not even from afar. I mean the thought that might even look appropriate painted on the recently plastered blind wall that you'll find up beyond my extra door: "Happiness is reminiscence."

Those Whom I Would Like to Meet Again: An Introduction

Salinger wrote a story called "Seymour: An Introduction." Seymour Glass, the narrator's brother—who didn't actually exist, but then existence isn't always a requirement for brothers—committed suicide in another story while vacationing with his wife in an oceanside hotel room smelling of veal and nail polish. When Seymour prepares to go swimming with a small girl staying in the same hotel, no one—neither the other beachgoers, nor anyone reading the story for the first time—suspect that he will shoot himself at the end of the story. That's the way a story's ending should be—unpredictable. Perhaps it seems to the reader that she will indeed read a story about a perfect day for catching bananafish: "He unrolled the towel he had used over his eyes, spread it out on the sand, and then laid the folded robe on top of it. He bent over, picked up the float, and secured it under his right arm. Then, with his left hand, he took Sybil's hand. The two started to walk down to the ocean." I really do think that great literature has died. Which is why ending a story with death has fallen out of fashion. Almost all contemporary art is intended to help us forget death, after all.

All of those whom I would like to meet again (excepting Seymour) really do exist. I like to remember them when I have a moment to myself—now, for example. I bought food for supper, because here, in the summerhouse, there's a kitchen. I went swimming twice—strange, it's the beginning of August, and the water in the sea is sixty-four degrees. Tomorrow it's supposed to be horribly windy. The smell of seaweed will penetrate the pinewoods. The waves will break in crests, and like in the famous Lithuanian artist's painting, splash the initials MKČ (Mikalojus Konstantinas Čiurlionis) on the water. I'll walk barefoot on damp sand that's like minnow spawn thrown out on the beach. And now I'm waiting for a friend to arrive. In the evening we'll watch a bad movie starring a good actor—Mickey Rourke, having emerged from the quagmire of alcohol and drugs, plays a wrestler. In his youth, he worked out his anger boxing, incidentally, in the same state where Seymour killed himself. Everything in the world, or almost everything, is connected.

When you're waiting for the arrival of a very close friend or loved one, you usually do have some idea where she is and what she's doing. I could call her, of course, but why bother, when I can see her so clearly? At a log-built donut shop and convenience store, next to the freeway, not even having reached Kryžkalnis yet. The grass at the side of the road is beginning to brown. There are colored inserts from the Sunday paper and plastic bottles scattered around. Ideally, the car radio isn't turned on; worst-case scenario, it's "Pretty woman, walking down the street," or "I can't get no satisfaction, I can't get no . . ." My friend looks at a bottle of brandy for a long time, but she resists and buys kvass, a donut, and some real wax candles poured by local craftspeople—one in the shape of an angel, the other of a phallus. She'll be here in approximately an hour and a half. After parking her car in the lot, across the little lawn, directly across from the window at which I'm sitting, she'll walk straight through the grass rather than up the sidewalk and around, saving herself approximately two meters, a Parliament cigarette clenched in her teeth all the while: "You couldn't come out and help?" she'll say. "Didn't you see my hands were full? Oh, Tadas called from his 'sports camp.' The toilet's in another building, so he and his roommate pee into a mineral water bottle. I brought him the icing from a donut, towels, gym shoes, and clean bedding, because nothing dries there. You won't mind if he spends the night here? With his friend? Yesterday someone stole a hundred litai from them, and their gym shoes too." And she'll kick the pink crocuses by the door, but by the time she's finished scattering around the clothes, towels, and mattresses she brought along for the weekend, by the time she's adorned the dresser with that framed black-and-white photo of a soldier she takes everywhere (I think of it as a portable Tomb of the Unknown Soldier), as well as her prescription glasses (-10.00 / -6.00), by the time she's poured herself some brandy from the bottle I've left on the table, by the time she's announced that people her age just aren't cut out for driving three hundred kilometers a day (yesterday she was all the way at the other end of Lithuania, at a funeral), by the time she thinks to have another smoke, her story about the funeral she just attended will have begun to break apart and die away, until it finally sputters out. In the dusk of the room I'll soon see only my friend's bare knees, the red point of her cigarette, and her six gesticulating arms. Dusk is my favorite time of day: sounds become muffled, less shrill; the cellophane of the air turns to flannel; ponds begin to reflect the netherworld; things turn into other versions of themselves; and characters from novels pour into the streets . . . I don't know where they come from, but they float about as quietly as sentences. "Now, that's how he'll take two hectares of land away from me," my friend will say, pointing at the refrigerator with her middle finger. "As far as I'm concerned, if he couldn't help carry the coffin yesterday, he shouldn't get the land—for that reason alone! The coffin was hardly heavy. When he got sick, my uncle turned from an oak to stewed rhubarb."

Whoever will or won't get those two hectares will have to remain anonymous to me for now. I'll have missed a good portion of the story by getting distracted by thoughts of how it happened that this woman became my best friend. A friend who, like the others I would like to meet again, is impossible to write about objectively, because love gets in the way. Salinger isn't the only one who noticed this contradiction; *Seymour: An Introduction* has an epigraph from Kafka: " . . . I write about them with steadfast love (even now, while I write it down, this, too, becomes false) but varying ability, and this varying ability does not hit off the real actors loudly and correctly but loses itself dully in this love that will never be satisfied with the ability and therefore thinks it is protecting the actors by preventing this ability from exercising itself."

I could have spent my weekend alone in the quiet, but I invited her here, and I suspect I'll have to put Salinger aside on the windowsill for the duration. The only things my friend has ever read are Zoshchenko's stories, and those not very carefully. When she needs to express herself, she resorts to Russian; she came late to Lithuanian. She's the sort of person who constantly changes channels while watching television, clicking away at the remote control; I can't stand that. (We'll go to bed without watching *The Wrestler*; it's obvious what a *shornik*, a scumbag, Rourke is, she'll say.) Her expenses never correspond to her income: she used to say that God had created too little money for the world, so she was borrowing it from the devil. She has no concept of the boundaries of "decent" conversation, crossing them at will. ("If I had to choose between oral sex or jellied carp, I'd go with the fish.") She's always playing with words, switching them around, wrong-footing you at just the right moment. ("The exception disproves the rule!") She likes to steal amusing signs from public places. The most valuable item in her collection is a sign she took from a changing room at a swimming pool: "Please refrain from using the hairdryers for hair anywhere but on your head." She's scheduled to have a valve replaced in her heart this year. She's still waiting, though; the same way I'd wait in a store for them to exchange a pair of shoes for one that's my size. She's always imagined she'd die the way her grandfather did. From a heart attack. Playing solitaire on a glassed-in veranda in the evening light. And, in the garden beyond the glass, as on a computer screen, the neighbor's grandchildren running about. Rain water in a bucket stirred by a fleck of dust. Winter apples strewn here and there by the windowsill. Three zucchini crocodiles and a fattened pumpkin lying on the nearby couch. Her knees bending slowly, she starts sliding sideways from her wicker chair. Her startled cat leaps from her lap into eternity, while a card falls out of her relaxing fingers.

I knew a lawyer in Chicago who smoked the same cigarettes as my friend—Parliaments. Every Sunday, dressed in a brown suit and a white shirt, and carrying a cane, he would come to a pseudo-Lithuanian restaurant where I worked. When people say that you can find every culture in the world in America, I always say, "You mean, you can find every culture's *surrogate* there." And on Sundays I used to fill in for a Lithuanian student who worked in that supposedly Lithuanian restaurant. The waitresses said that the lawyer had gone bankrupt. He would barely touch the duck he always ordered. The man would cut his bird up into little pieces, as if there were a diamond ring hidden in the roast, and then, after a half hour of this, with a disappointed look on his face, he would smoke a cigarette—always sitting at the same table in the smoking section. Once, without even finishing his cigarette, he leaped up, threw some cash on the table, and ran out into the street to hail a yellow cab. I'd already worked about three Sunday shifts in that restaurant before I found out that the lawyer was blind. I'd like to meet him again, too. I'd like to meet him again the way I sometimes want to get to the end of a movie.

Another blind person I'd like to meet again is my uncle. He

started going blind when he was still a student learning Spanish and English at the Pedagogical Institute. He didn't finish at the Institute, because back then there weren't any tape recorders, computers, or other audio tools accessible to the blind. He went to a clinic in Odessa, and there they did the first operation—they took some skin from his lower lip and patched it over one of his eyeballs. There was an Armenian in the ward who couldn't distinguish between gender and person in foreign languages; when he went to fetch wine, speaking Russian, he'd refer to himself in the third person feminine. When Uncle's turn came to fetch the wine, he got lost. With one covered eye and a swollen lip. While he was walking through the courtyard of the dilapidated hospital, he saw a half-naked woman standing in an open window, leaning against the window frame. Uncle even thought that the famous Odessa Catacombs started there. "She might have been naked, that guide to the Catacombs," he said many years later, "but I don't remember seeing a bit of her treasure, the center of her life, if you know what I mean, below the windowsill. When I went on my way, a desert that wasn't on the map of Ukraine spread out on the other side of the building." Uncle didn't carry a white cane and walked the streets of his hometown quickly, seeing everything with the eyes of memory. But, once, he knocked over a baby carriage standing on the little bridge—knocked it over with its occupant still on board. The child's mother for some reason called Uncle impotent, and the carriage floated down the creek to the Nevėžis. The boy survived, and was carried back to shore on the back of a swan, later becoming an honorary citizen of that town; he now works at the Ministry of Transport. Uncle and I still exchange gifts from time to time. My last gift to him was a Catalan woman singing "Bésame Mucho." I went up to her after a concert at an old manor house. I told her about Uncle's unfinished studies in Spanish, and she, without even waiting for the end of my story, made a gift of that song to him by singing it right there into my cell phone. Now when he calls, they sing together. On my end there's blindingly white Catalan teeth lighting up the telephone, while, at the other end of the country, there's my uncle: sagging pajamas, wool socks, and a room without light. Why would it need light? Light had no function there. Music now means the same to my uncle as light does to others. But when

I was three years old, Uncle could still see. ("Don't worry," he says, "I can still remember how tea turns lighter in the cup when you put some lemon in it.") He used to like to photograph women, particularly those who never seemed to change with age; chess pieces on a board, if they were in stalemate; and pale sprouts breaking through the sidewalk. Shouting "Hola!" he used to pick me up and toss me into the air, using only one hand, all the way to the ceiling, which at the time I thought of as a convenient wooden sky that my parents had decided to rent. Of all the small children tossed into the air with only one hand, there's only one I'd like to meet again: my daughter, as a small child. An egotistic wish, as she was someone who loved me unconditionally. In the kitchen, in Panevėžys, she would open the cabinet door and play with the dried beans. Watching her from the side, I liked to dissemble the girl into her component parts. The hair was from her grandmother (the other one); the smile was from that portrait of my mother as a little girl; the bones and logic were from her father; the voice from me; the ability to think spatially from God. They call God the Great Designer, because he created everything. My daughter decided to follow in His footsteps as a designer. Now she's grown up; when I look at her from the side I no longer take her apart. And I suspect that she has someone who loves her unconditionally. On her birthday, this fellow texts her, telling her where in Vilnius he's buried this year's presents. With a silver flour scoop, my daughter digs a little box out of the ground containing toys made just for her by the young man in question: a lantern with cats and mice hugging, umbrellas designed to shield your head from fear, and nonexistent birds of paradise engraved on its glass. And a carousel that actually turns; in place of chairs it had halved walnut shells bearing sugared almonds. Sometimes he includes a note as well.

On the subject of unconditional lovers, I should also mention a particular man from my own biography. I was attracted to him in the same way a patient can get attracted to a psychiatrist—and vice versa . . . I think that, while he was with me, the world seemed brighter to him, more open, a series of discrete, colorful images, as though seen from the cars of a train traveling at great speed. We had no future as a couple: we both lived in other worlds, whereas a happy couple should live in this one. I always enjoyed something he used to say: "There are only two occasions on which I could actually say I'm happy, in this life—when I'm drunk, or when I come up with a new idea." Once, he went to a conference in Prague. After the conference, along with his colleagues, he drank several pints of Budweiser, and I should mention that he had the silly habit of sleeping in the nude whenever possible. Unlike me, he didn't associate a naked body with the soul; it's just a material, he used to say, like clay, asbestos, or silk. Anyway, during the night, in his monk's cell of a hotel room, this friend of mine got out of bed, took two steps, turned left to enter the bathroom, opened the door, went inside, and then, leaving the bathroom a moment later, he took *another* turn to the left, after which he slammed the door behind him. He opened his eyes in a long corridor: dim lights protruded from frosted glass lotuses, and a red runner stretched to nowhere, like something unspooling out of his dreams. There weren't a lot of options. The first: knock on the door next to his, in which a conference participant from Poland—not always friendly to our people, but truly Christian—was sleeping. The second: wrap himself up in the carpet and present himself like Cleopatra to the Anthonys at the front desk. He bent down and felt it—no, the carpet was too stiff and too long. And yet, the woman working the registration desk that night gave him his key without even a second look—reaching out and dropping it into his outstretched palm (my friend had used a brochure about Prague's old town as a fig leaf).

Shortly after we broke up, I returned from an overnight trip to Poland. I was carrying a heavy bag down a railway platform. I don't know why I still haven't bought a wheeled suitcase. And here's another personal fault of mine, to add to the list: whenever I get upset—or, should I say, agitated—whatever I'm wearing at the time becomes etched permanently into my memory, remaining perfectly clear even after decades. So, I was hauling my bag through the station and suddenly felt it getting lighter behind me, and rising into the air . . . I turned around, and there, on the platform, sleepy-eyed, was the man for whom the world looked, when he was with me, like bright flashes of countryside seen from a speeding train. "You're meeting someone here?" I asked him. "I am," he said, looking into my eyes. And I looked into his, but all I saw were my beige stockings, twisted not once but twice; my face bedraggled from two border crossings; the beret covering my greasy hair; and the bandage on the heel of my right foot. And if my bag were to continue the story, the events on the platform might play out like so: "The man carried me to a car and threw me into its empty trunk. But my owner lifted me out again. 'Don't be silly,' the man said. 'It's Christmas, look at how many people are waiting at the trolleybus stop, let me take you to Panevėžys.' The man got into the driver's seat, flicking the toy spider dangling from his rearview mirror, while the woman walked off, heading for the bus station. Waiting in line for a ticket, she put me down on the muddy floor and then fell right on top of me; I expected my ribs—made up of books, boxes, cans, and shoes—to tear through the skin at my sides. I remembered then that fifteen hours before, at the departures tracks, a different man had seen my owner off. They kissed on the platform. I suppose she must have thought that a different man unexpectedly meeting her on her return was some sort of sin?" I thought about how I would behave now. I would probably have gone to hell with him, that man for whom the naked body, unrelated to the soul, was just another material, like so many others—clay, asbestos, silk. But, then, who really knows where we board the train to hell. Where its tracks begin, where they end, or what's waiting there?

There are people with whom it wouldn't be frightening to travel to hell. One of them is my cousin; for all I know, he's already been there. The conductor of the universe. He doesn't have the time for such long trips anymore. He's working off his debts. He despises wealth, but he can't stand to live anywhere "cramped." When he bought his apartment, he borrowed a portion of the money in cash from an American Lithuanian, an old lady who'd been using him as a free computer repair service for years. He'd swear a blue streak about what he went through in her place; sweeping aside all the velvet-framed pictures in of her grandchildren and great-grandchildren in order to reach the keyboard, and then being forced to listen to her endless stories of their victorious college baseball teams . . . "How are you planning to pay her back all that money?" I asked. "Oh, you're such a worrier . . . How, how? I'll tell you how: the way large sums of money are exchanged in the movies . . . In a suitcase, in rows, wrapped in little packs." Back when he had a jeep, we used to drive out to the swamps. My cousin would drag along a suitcase full of unwanted possessions or other leftovers from remodeling his new apartment—broken skis, unused bits of floorboard, computer monitor boxes, other pieces of cardboard, and stacks of paper—dropping them at the nearby dump. But the swamps next to Trakai have been fixed up nicely now. Without even stepping off the boardwalk you can reach a thin, nearly-transparent birch, bend its trunk down all the way to the ground, let it go, and watch it spring back into its original position, since its roots have fixed themselves into the greenery at the bottom of the reservoir. There's a floating observation post built out on the lake. We'd spread cheese, bread, and tea on the bench and watch, as people say, "junipers growing gin." There's never many people there, even in July. Toward evening we met two men from Sweden with a movie camera; they hoped to find some rare birds, perhaps a curlew, in that landscape already browned like a poor-quality photograph. On the narrow path, we passed a silent family whose members seemed as though they'd already been bored with each other centuries ago: a mother, two teenaged boys behind her, and father leading a Great Dane. The dog's muzzle looked like the bars of a jail; I pictured them all trapped inside. By the time we'd gotten back to dry land, by now the only visitors in sight, my cousin was only carrying his knapsack. "You left your suitcase back there," I said. "What will you use to carry your next load of garbage to the dump?" "What, what. Oh, you're such a worrier. I don't need it anymore. I've finally dug my way out. There's nothing left to throw away." Whenever I remember returning from somewhere, I take leave of it all over again. I imagine how the place went on, after me, objectively. "The southern part of the reserve extends over 207 hectares, in which there are four small lakes: Baluošas, Piliškių, Bevardis, and Ilgelis. These little lakes are in fact the remnants of what was once a single, larger lake. The Dumblė, which has turned into a bog, lies to the north of Ilgelis. All the lakes of the Varnikai reserve are fed by the swamps surrounding them. The swamp water rises nearly a meter higher than the level of Bernardinų (Luka) Lake. The excess water flows through irrigation canals to Bernardinų Lake, so the lower edges of the marsh have been reclaimed and are now grown over with bushes, while the highland is covered in pine and birch. Indigenous fauna has not been extensively researched, but local lore suggests that many rare species of bird breed in this area." And, as far as flora, if you were to dive beneath the chill waters of the lake with a movie camera, you'd find everything there: canes, rushes, cattails . . . While in the formless, saprophytic mass of decomposing plants and animals, you'd also find an abundance of embedded trash, the largest of which is an old suitcase. Inside it—an old lady, sliced up into pieces. Judging from the two gold rings on the nameless lady's finger, she was an American Lithuanian. Inscriptions: "To Peter, With Love. To Birute, With Love. Detroit, 1950." I'd like to meet my cousin again, too. But how? "How, how! Don't be such a worrier. I live, after all, in every one of your stories."

As for the old ladies I've met, I'd like to meet almost all of them again. Particularly the ones in Kieślowski's movies. With purses of cracked oilskin hanging on their arms, they go up to dumpsters, stand on their tiptoes, and—reaching over the lip with great difficulty—try to get their empty bottles down into the hole, holding these by their tips; they push and shove the way men would shove a heavy rowboat into the water. (This year, by reducing pensions and other such expenses by ten percent, it will be possible for the government to save 510 million. "People don't earn pensions; they earn the possibility of getting one.") Come to think of it, I'd like very much to meet one particular old lady who got written up in the newspapers— but they say she doesn't let anyone near. She's been afraid of people for sixty years now, since the day she was raped by soldiers. Although she was very pretty, she stayed in a remote village to live in poverty with her half-witted brother, who liked to play the accordion on Sundays. And we know all about those village Sundays, don't we—a hard-boiled egg steaming; a fly banging into the window; a ray of sunshine, as if it were alive, crawling out from behind the clouds and cleaving the room in two. Tarkovsky could have had his soundman record a tearing cobweb in a remote village, just to check his equipment. Last summer I checked for myself whether this business of hearing a cobweb tear was even possible, given the exploitation of this conceit by writers . . . not least this one. (A cobweb tears like wet gauze, and the sound can indeed be heard, by ordinary ears, in complete silence . . . if you aren't thinking about anything else at that moment.) That old lady never went anywhere, except the cemetery, to visit her father and mother's graves. When she had tidied the perennials, she would leave her little rake behind a fence and, before heading for home, she would lay down on the loosened soil, the way others would lay on a memory-foam mattress. When some drunken thieves broke down her cottage door, looking for hidden pension money, and beat her brother savagely, she tried to bandage his head with rags, but by the next day he had gone cold. The old lady never even reported the misfortune to the village officials. She was afraid. She wrote a note, put it into the open case of the accordion, and left it on the road. I'd write about this old lady in more detail if someone asked me to compose a text for the national dictation contest. I know what a text like that needs: love for the homeland, a bit of history and hope. Well, and some special grammatical forms, so that people don't forget that the accusative inflection for nouns gets an *ogonek* (little tail), and pronominal numerals and adjectives even get two (for example, *per Antrąjį pasaulinį karą* ["during the Second World War"]). As far as consonant assimilation, a voiced consonant next to an unvoiced one gets muffled (she stayed to live in poverty with a halfwit).

"Are you even listening?" my friend asked, turning on the light and instantly destroying all the twilight people who'd been distracting me. "I have no intention of going to court, but he won't get the land. Let's go to bed. We'll skip *The Wrestler*. It's obvious what a *sbornika* Rourke is."

The next day, on the beach, on the sand, my friend unrolled the towel she had used over her eyes (-10.00 / -6.00), spread it out on the sand, and laid her robe on top of it. Flashing her nails, freshly polished that morning in the summerhouse, she unrolled the foil from the veal sandwiches she had brought yesterday. (In Vilnius, she gets her meat from a farmer.) Then, with her left hand, she took Tadas's right, and the two walked toward the ocean. People bathed by wading in only halfway, and everyone likewise seemed to be holding smaller children by the hand. Before stepping into the water, my friend turned around and waved to me—at the groin of her bathing suit, a graying tuft of pubic hair stuck out. Tadas climbed up on the float, and my friend pushed him deeper—lightly and softly . . . When she returns she'll undoubtedly pause by the changing station and tear off the announcement I already read on the way over here— "Table for sale. Imtation marbel. French. Bonparte III period." It was terribly windy. The red flag warning of dangerous swimming conditions was out. A woman wearing a jacket on top of her bathing suit, her hands formed into a cone, was standing on her tiptoes out in the water, hysterically calling to someone to rescue her, but the wind kept returning her screams like loose paper. Vacationers walked out of the sea sinking into the wet sand that resembles minnow's spawn. The crests of the waves roared as they broke, the spray splattering the initials MKČ on the water.

. . . For Milda Katinaitė, Česlov's. Do you know who you are to me, like all others I would like to meet again? A nation. With a replacement heart valve or two. A nation whose banks lend money in the middle of the night, and without interest. A nation with treaties to sign. Full of cafés and restaurants. Concerts. (When you bought us tickets to see Joe Cocker, I was surprised that you knew who he was.) And a kitchen in you, somewhere, in which we once ate cabbage pie. Full of urgent crises too, for which, without regret, I will set even the most interesting of books aside, leaving it on a windowsill for a whole weekend. And of course with gold reserves—the locket you gave me, which I'm wearing now, is inscribed with the initials "D.G.": (not yours, and don't imagine that they're the president's, either). A nation with its own laws, its own justice: "As far as I'm concerned, if he couldn't help carry the coffin, he shouldn't get the land—for that reason alone! The coffin was hardly heavy. When he got sick, my uncle turned from an oak to stewed rhubarb." A nation dotted with emergency telephones in November (for example, on train-station platforms) for the use of those who may be considering suicide. Free seminars on business, sex, and knitting. A military too, destroyers, spreading a cloud of melancholy across the world. Cell-phone towers, so that I can reach you even when I don't know where you are. And a flag, flying high, made out of graying pubic hair.

" . . . I write about them with steadfast love (even now, while I write it down, this too becomes false) but varying ability, and this varying ability does not hit off the real actors loudly and correctly but loses itself dully in this love that will never be satisfied with the ability and therefore thinks it is protecting the actors by preventing this ability from exercising itself." (I think you can really only translate good prose smoothly when you're a bit drunk. And during a full moon.)

And among all those whom I'd like to meet again, I'll also single out the man who translated Salinger into Lithuanian. We'd discuss art a bit, as we did once before. He told me I know nothing about contemporary art. Perhaps because I'd flippantly asked, "Could you explain why salt in a shoe is art, but in a sock is uncleanliness?" He translated Salinger at a farmstead in a small village. When he was working, and decided he'd earned one of his rare breaks, he went out to stand in the yard on the knotweed and eat a sandwich. In the light of the moon, cold stars and warm crumbs of bread would fall. In his head, like a thousand cobwebs tearing at once, he would hear Bach, perhaps the piece used in *Solaris*. Casting down his eyes, looking at the grass as if it were a battlefield, he would try to rally the army of English words at his command, to force it—all of it—to desert their posts, to join up with his native language, and then, standing to attention, without regret, condemn all their prepositions to death, leading them up to the guillotine, changing them into six inflections and attempting to preserve their rhythm with nothing much more than intuition to guide him . . . until he would get giddy from the sound of the thundering hooves of the multiplying participles, half-participles, and gerunds, until he would get stuck in the convolvulus of two syntaxes and stand, stunned, in front of the already tangible, seemingly under control, but secretly growing chasm of equivalence as it yawned before him once more. "A great part of the moonlight would fall next to the barn and the barn door. I guarantee that if someone had written the very name of God on that door, it would be impossible to read because of the moonlight poured over it."

"I don't know where this sentence came from," he admitted to me. "Is it mine or not? So long as I don't know, I have to say, it intimidates me more than a little . . ."

Giedra Radvilavičiūtė studied philology and literature at Vilnius University. She has worked as a teacher and as an editor, and her work has been published in numerous journals. She has published two books of her writing in Lithuania.

Elizabeth Novickas studied rhetoric and fine printing at the University of Illinois in Urbana-Champaign. Her next project, a translation of Petra Cvirka's *Frank Kruk*, has received support from the National Endowment for the Arts.

◨

SELECTED DALKEY ARCHIVE TITLES

MICHAL AJVAZ, *The Golden Age.*
The Other City.
PIERRE ALBERT-BIROT, *Grabinoulor.*
YUZ ALESHKOVSKY, *Kangaroo.*
FELIPE ALFAU, *Chromos.*
Locos.
IVAN ÂNGELO, *The Celebration.*
The Tower of Glass.
ANTÓNIO LOBO ANTUNES, *Knowledge of Hell.*
The Splendor of Portugal.
ALAIN ARIAS-MISSON, *Theatre of Incest.*
JOHN ASHBERY AND JAMES SCHUYLER,
A Nest of Ninnies.
ROBERT ASHLEY, *Perfect Lives.*
GABRIELA AVIGUR-ROTEM, *Heatwave*
and Crazy Birds.
DJUNA BARNES, *Ladies Almanack.*
Ryder.
JOHN BARTH, *LETTERS.*
Sabbatical.
DONALD BARTHELME, *The King.*
Paradise.
SVETISLAV BASARA, *Chinese Letter.*
MIQUEL BAUÇÀ, *The Siege in the Room.*
RENÉ BELLETTO, *Dying.*
MAREK BIEŃCZYK, *Transparency.*
ANDREI BITOV, *Pushkin House.*
ANDREJ BLATNIK, *You Do Understand.*
LOUIS PAUL BOON, *Chapel Road.*
My Little War.
Summer in Termuren.
ROGER BOYLAN, *Killoyle.*
IGNÁCIO DE LOYOLA BRANDÃO,
Anonymous Celebrity.
Zero.
BONNIE BREMSER, *Troia: Mexican Memoirs.*
CHRISTINE BROOKE-ROSE, *Amalgamemnon.*
BRIGID BROPHY, *In Transit.*
GERALD L. BRUNS, *Modern Poetry and*
the Idea of Language.
GABRIELLE BURTON, *Heartbreak Hotel.*
MICHEL BUTOR, *Degrees.*
Mobile.
G. CABRERA INFANTE, *Infante's Inferno.*
Three Trapped Tigers.
JULIETA CAMPOS,
The Fear of Losing Eurydice.
ANNE CARSON, *Eros the Bittersweet.*
ORLY CASTEL-BLOOM, *Dolly City.*
LOUIS-FERDINAND CÉLINE, *Castle to Castle.*
Conversations with Professor Y.
London Bridge.
Normance.
North.
Rigadoon.
MARIE CHAIX, *The Laurels of Lake Constance.*
HUGO CHARTERIS, *The Tide Is Right.*
ERIC CHEVILLARD, *Demolishing Nisard.*
MARC CHOLODENKO, *Mordechai Schamz.*
JOSHUA COHEN, *Witz.*
EMILY HOLMES COLEMAN, *The Shutter*
of Snow.
ROBERT COOVER, *A Night at the Movies.*
STANLEY CRAWFORD, *Log of the S.S. The*
Mrs Unguentine.
Some Instructions to My Wife.
RENÉ CREVEL, *Putting My Foot in It.*
RALPH CUSACK, *Cadenza.*
NICHOLAS DELBANCO, *The Count of Concord.*
Sherbrookes.
NIGEL DENNIS, *Cards of Identity.*

PETER DIMOCK, *A Short Rhetoric for*
Leaving the Family.
ARIEL DORFMAN, *Konfidenz.*
COLEMAN DOWELL,
Island People.
Too Much Flesh and Jabez.
ARKADII DRAGOMOSHCHENKO, *Dust.*
RIKKI DUCORNET, *The Complete*
Butcher's Tales.
The Fountains of Neptune.
The Jade Cabinet.
Phosphor in Dreamland.
WILLIAM EASTLAKE, *The Bamboo Bed.*
Castle Keep.
Lyric of the Circle Heart.
JEAN ECHENOZ, *Chopin's Move.*
STANLEY ELKIN, *A Bad Man.*
Criers and Kibitzers, Kibitzers
and Criers.
The Dick Gibson Show.
The Franchiser.
The Living End.
Mrs. Ted Bliss.
FRANÇOIS EMMANUEL, *Invitation to a*
Voyage.
SALVADOR ESPRIU, *Ariadne in the*
Grotesque Labyrinth.
LESLIE A. FIEDLER, *Love and Death in*
the American Novel.
JUAN FILLOY, *Op Oloop.*
ANDY FITCH, *Pop Poetics.*
GUSTAVE FLAUBERT, *Bouvard and Pécuchet.*
KASS FLEISHER, *Talking out of School.*
FORD MADOX FORD,
The March of Literature.
JON FOSSE, *Aliss at the Fire.*
Melancholy.
MAX FRISCH, *I'm Not Stiller.*
Man in the Holocene.
CARLOS FUENTES, *Christopher Unborn.*
Distant Relations.
Terra Nostra.
Where the Air Is Clear.
TAKEHIKO FUKUNAGA, *Flowers of Grass.*
WILLIAM GADDIS, *J R.*
The Recognitions.
JANICE GALLOWAY, *Foreign Parts.*
The Trick Is to Keep Breathing.
WILLIAM H. GASS, *Cartesian Sonata*
and Other Novellas.
Finding a Form.
A Temple of Texts.
The Tunnel.
Willie Masters' Lonesome Wife.
GÉRARD GAVARRY, *Hoppla! 1 2 3.*
ETIENNE GILSON,
The Arts of the Beautiful.
Forms and Substances in the Arts.
C. S. GISCOMBE, *Giscome Road.*
Here.
DOUGLAS GLOVER, *Bad News of the Heart.*
WITOLD GOMBROWICZ,
A Kind of Testament.
PAULO EMÍLIO SALES GOMES, *P's Three*
Women.
GEORGI GOSPODINOV, *Natural Novel.*
JUAN GOYTISOLO, *Count Julian.*
Juan the Landless.
Makbara.
Marks of Identity.

FOR A FULL LIST OF PUBLICATIONS, VISIT:
www.dalkeyarchive.com

SELECTED DALKEY ARCHIVE TITLES

HENRY GREEN, *Back.*
Blindness.
Concluding.
Doting.
Nothing.
JACK GREEN, *Fire the Bastards!*
JIŘÍ GRUŠA, *The Questionnaire.*
MELA HARTWIG, *Am I a Redundant*
Human Being?
JOHN HAWKES, *The Passion Artist.*
Whistlejacket.
ELIZABETH HEIGHWAY, ED., *Contemporary*
Georgian Fiction.
ALEKSANDAR HEMON, ED.,
Best European Fiction.
AIDAN HIGGINS, *Balcony of Europe.*
Blind Man's Bluff
Bornholm Night-Ferry.
Flotsam and Jetsam.
Langrishe, Go Down.
Scenes from a Receding Past.
KEIZO HINO, *Isle of Dreams.*
KAZUSHI HOSAKA, *Plainsong.*
ALDOUS HUXLEY, *Antic Hay.*
Crome Yellow.
Point Counter Point.
Those Barren Leaves.
Time Must Have a Stop.
NAOYUKI II, *The Shadow of a Blue Cat.*
GERT JONKE, *The Distant Sound.*
Geometric Regional Novel.
Homage to Czerny.
The System of Vienna.
JACQUES JOUET, *Mountain R.*
Savage.
Upstaged.
MIEKO KANAI, *The Word Book.*
YORAM KANIUK, *Life on Sandpaper.*
HUGH KENNER, *Flaubert.*
Joyce and Beckett: The Stoic Comedians.
Joyce's Voices.
DANILO KIŠ, *The Attic.*
Garden, Ashes.
The Lute and the Scars
Psalm 44.
A Tomb for Boris Davidovich.
ANITA KONKKA, *A Fool's Paradise.*
GEORGE KONRÁD, *The City Builder.*
TADEUSZ KONWICKI, *A Minor Apocalypse.*
The Polish Complex.
MENIS KOUMANDAREAS, *Koula.*
ELAINE KRAF, *The Princess of 72nd Street.*
JIM KRUSOE, *Iceland.*
AYŞE KULIN, *Farewell: A Mansion in*
Occupied Istanbul.
EMILIO LASCANO TEGUI, *On Elegance*
While Sleeping.
ERIC LAURRENT, *Do Not Touch.*
VIOLETTE LEDUC, *La Bâtarde.*
EDOUARD LEVÉ, *Autoportrait.*
Suicide.
MARIO LEVI, *Istanbul Was a Fairy Tale.*
DEBORAH LEVY, *Billy and Girl.*
JOSÉ LEZAMA LIMA, *Paradiso.*
ROSA LIKSOM, *Dark Paradise.*
OSMAN LINS, *Avalovara.*
The Queen of the Prisons of Greece.
ALF MAC LOCHLAINN,
The Corpus in the Library.
Out of Focus.
RON LOEWINSOHN, *Magnetic Field(s).*
MINA LOY, *Stories and Essays of Mina Loy.*

D. KEITH MANO, *Take Five.*
MICHELINE AHARONIAN MARCOM,
The Mirror in the Well.
BEN MARCUS,
The Age of Wire and String.
WALLACE MARKFIELD,
Teitlebaum's Window.
To an Early Grave.
DAVID MARKSON, *Reader's Block.*
Wittgenstein's Mistress.
CAROLE MASO, *AVA.*
LADISLAV MATEJKA AND KRYSTYNA
POMORSKA, EDS.,
Readings in Russian Poetics:
Formalist and Structuralist Views.
HARRY MATHEWS, *Cigarettes.*
The Conversions.
The Human Country: New and
Collected Stories.
The Journalist.
My Life in CIA.
Singular Pleasures.
The Sinking of the Odradek
Stadium.
Tlooth.
JOSEPH MCELROY,
Night Soul and Other Stories.
ABDELWAHAB MEDDEB, *Talismano.*
GERHARD MEIER, *Isle of the Dead.*
HERMAN MELVILLE, *The Confidence-Man.*
AMANDA MICHALOPOULOU, *I'd Like.*
STEVEN MILLHAUSER, *The Barnum Museum.*
In the Penny Arcade.
RALPH J. MILLS, JR., *Essays on Poetry.*
MOMUS, *The Book of Jokes.*
CHRISTINE MONTALBETTI, *The Origin of Man.*
Western.
OLIVE MOORE, *Spleen.*
NICHOLAS MOSLEY, *Accident.*
Assassins.
Catastrophe Practice.
Experience and Religion.
A Garden of Trees.
Hopeful Monsters.
Imago Bird.
Impossible Object.
Inventing God.
Judith.
Look at the Dark.
Natalie Natalia.
Serpent.
Time at War.
WARREN MOTTE,
Fables of the Novel: French Fiction
since 1990.
Fiction Now: The French Novel in
the 21st Century.
Oulipo: A Primer of Potential
Literature.
GERALD MURNANE, *Barley Patch.*
Inland.
YVES NAVARRE, *Our Share of Time.*
Sweet Tooth.
DOROTHY NELSON, *In Night's City.*
Tar and Feathers.
ESHKOL NEVO, *Homesick.*
WILFRIDO D. NOLLEDO, *But for the Lovers.*
FLANN O'BRIEN, *At Swim-Two-Birds.*
The Best of Myles.
The Dalkey Archive.
The Hard Life.
The Poor Mouth.

SELECTED DALKEY ARCHIVE TITLES

The Third Policeman.
CLAUDE OLLIER, *The Mise-en-Scène.*
Wert and the Life Without End.
GIOVANNI ORELLI, *Walaschek's Dream.*
PATRIK OUŘEDNÍK, *Europeana.*
The Opportune Moment, 1855.
BORIS PAHOR, *Necropolis.*
FERNANDO DEL PASO, *News from the Empire.*
Palinuro of Mexico.
ROBERT PINGET, *The Inquisitory.*
Mahu or The Material.
Trio.
MANUEL PUIG, *Betrayed by Rita Hayworth.*
The Buenos Aires Affair.
Heartbreak Tango.
RAYMOND QUENEAU, *The Last Days.*
Odile.
Pierrot Mon Ami.
Saint Glinglin.
ANN QUIN, *Berg.*
Passages.
Three.
Tripticks.
ISHMAEL REED, *The Free-Lance Pallbearers.*
The Last Days of Louisiana Red.
Ishmael Reed: The Plays.
Juice!
Reckless Eyeballing.
The Terrible Threes.
The Terrible Twos.
Yellow Back Radio Broke-Down.
JASIA REICHARDT, *15 Journeys Warsaw
    to London.*
NOËLLE REVAZ, *With the Animals.*
JOÃO UBALDO RIBEIRO, *House of the
    Fortunate Buddhas.*
JEAN RICARDOU, *Place Names.*
RAINER MARIA RILKE, *The Notebooks of
    Malte Laurids Brigge.*
JULIÁN RÍOS, *The House of Ulysses.*
Larva: A Midsummer Night's Babel.
Poundemonium.
Procession of Shadows.
AUGUSTO ROA BASTOS, *I the Supreme.*
DANIËL ROBBERECHTS, *Arriving in Avignon.*
JEAN ROLIN, *The Explosion of the
    Radiator Hose.*
OLIVIER ROLIN, *Hotel Crystal.*
ALIX CLEO ROUBAUD, *Alix's Journal.*
JACQUES ROUBAUD, *The Form of a
    City Changes Faster, Alas, Than
    the Human Heart.*
The Great Fire of London.
Hortense in Exile.
Hortense Is Abducted.
The Loop.
Mathematics:
The Plurality of Worlds of Lewis.
The Princess Hoppy.
Some Thing Black.
RAYMOND ROUSSEL, *Impressions of Africa.*
VEDRANA RUDAN, *Night.*
STIG SÆTERBAKKEN, *Siamese.*
Self Control.
LYDIE SALVAYRE, *The Company of Ghosts.*
The Lecture.
The Power of Flies.
LUIS RAFAEL SÁNCHEZ,
    Macho Camacho's Beat.
SEVERO SARDUY, *Cobra & Maitreya.*

NATHALIE SARRAUTE,
Do You Hear Them?
Martereau.
The Planetarium.
ARNO SCHMIDT, *Collected Novellas.*
Collected Stories.
Nobodaddy's Children.
Two Novels.
ASAF SCHURR, *Motti.*
GAIL SCOTT, *My Paris.*
DAMION SEARLS, *What We Were Doing
    and Where We Were Going.*
JUNE AKERS SEESE,
Is This What Other Women Feel Too?
What Waiting Really Means.
BERNARD SHARE, *Inish.*
Transit.
VIKTOR SHKLOVSKY, *Bowstring.*
Knight's Move.
*A Sentimental Journey:
    Memoirs 1917–1922.*
Energy of Delusion: A Book on Plot.
Literature and Cinematography.
Theory of Prose.
Third Factory.
Zoo, or Letters Not about Love.
PIERRE SINIAC, *The Collaborators.*
KJERSTI A. SKOMSVOLD, *The Faster I Walk,
    the Smaller I Am.*
JOSEF ŠKVORECKÝ, *The Engineer of
    Human Souls.*
GILBERT SORRENTINO,
Aberration of Starlight.
Blue Pastoral.
Crystal Vision.
*Imaginative Qualities of Actual
    Things.*
Mulligan Stew.
Pack of Lies.
Red the Fiend.
The Sky Changes.
Something Said.
Splendide-Hôtel.
Steelwork.
Under the Shadow.
W. M. SPACKMAN, *The Complete Fiction.*
ANDRZEJ STASIUK, *Dukla.*
Fado.
GERTRUDE STEIN, *The Making of Americans.*
A Novel of Thank You.
LARS SVENDSEN, *A Philosophy of Evil.*
PIOTR SZEWC, *Annihilation.*
GONÇALO M. TAVARES, *Jerusalem.*
Joseph Walser's Machine.
*Learning to Pray in the Age of
    Technique.*
LUCIAN DAN TEODOROVICI,
    Our Circus Presents . . .
NIKANOR TERATOLOGEN, *Assisted Living.*
STEFAN THEMERSON, *Hobson's Island.*
The Mystery of the Sardine.
Tom Harris.
TAEKO TOMIOKA, *Building Waves.*
JOHN TOOMEY, *Sleepwalker.*
JEAN-PHILIPPE TOUSSAINT, *The Bathroom.*
Camera.
Monsieur.
Reticence.
Running Away.
Self-Portrait Abroad.
Television.
The Truth about Marie.

SELECTED DALKEY ARCHIVE TITLES

DUMITRU TSEPENEAG, *Hotel Europa.*
The Necessary Marriage.
Pigeon Post.
Vain Art of the Fugue.
ESTHER TUSQUETS, *Stranded.*
DUBRAVKA UGRESIC, *Lend Me Your Character.*
Thank You for Not Reading.
TOR ULVEN, *Replacement.*
MATI UNT, *Brecht at Night.*
Diary of a Blood Donor.
Things in the Night.
ÁLVARO URIBE AND OLIVIA SEARS, EDS.,
Best of Contemporary Mexican Fiction.
ELOY URROZ, *Friction.*
The Obstacles.
LUISA VALENZUELA, *Dark Desires and
the Others.*
He Who Searches.
PAUL VERHAEGHEN, *Omega Minor.*
AGLAJA VETERANYI, *Why the Child Is
Cooking in the Polenta.*
BORIS VIAN, *Heartsnatcher.*
LLORENÇ VILLALONGA, *The Dolls' Room.*
TOOMAS VINT, *An Unending Landscape.*
ORNELA VORPSI, *The Country Where No
One Ever Dies.*
AUSTRYN WAINHOUSE, *Hedyphagetica.*
CURTIS WHITE, *America's Magic Mountain.*
The Idea of Home.
Memories of My Father Watching TV.
Requiem.

DIANE WILLIAMS, *Excitability:
Selected Stories.*
Romancer Erector.
DOUGLAS WOOLF, *Wall to Wall.*
Ya! & John-Juan.
JAY WRIGHT, *Polynomials and Pollen.*
*The Presentable Art of Reading
Absence.*
PHILIP WYLIE, *Generation of Vipers.*
MARGUERITE YOUNG, *Angel in the Forest.*
Miss MacIntosh, My Darling.
REYOUNG, *Unbabbling.*
VLADO ŽABOT, *The Succubus.*
ZORAN ŽIVKOVIĆ, *Hidden Camera.*
LOUIS ZUKOFSKY, *Collected Fiction.*
VITOMIL ZUPAN, *Minuet for Guitar.*
SCOTT ZWIREN, *God Head.*